Slippery Things

Lane Baker

Edited by Lilly Penhall

Cover and Interior Design by Lilly Penhall

Interstellar Graphics

Front Cover Art by Jennifer MaHarry

Special Thanks to Bob Mathews and Victor Bumbalo

Table of Contents

This book is dedicated to Kevin Baker-Cross and Madalyn Lee Baker-Cross.

CHAPTER 1

Larissa Locke slouched in the awkwardly uncomfortable chair across the desk from Assistant Principal Walter Miller for about ninety seconds without either one saying so much as a word. Larissa could tell the administrator's eyes focused on her with laser-like precision, but she simply wasn't in the mood for eye contact.

"So, Larissa, was it your feces?" Mr. Miller asked for the third time in a row.

If he thought repeating the question was going to get a rise out of her, he had another thing coming. She could work a fierce poker face like the best of them, especially when someone was trying to rile her up.

After another twenty-or-so second stand-off, he droned on, "You know, for a stunt like this, normally I would suspend you. But after looking at your behavioral history this year, expulsion is not out of the question."

Larissa offered a faint shrug, as if to say, "Is that the best you can do?" Then she pretended to mull over the faded certificates on his wall and the gaudy pattern of the window curtains behind him.

"I'm really wondering what it was that made you act out in this way. What has Christy Carmichael ever done to you?" he implored.

This, of course, Larissa didn't answer either, but acted as though she suffered from a hearing disability. This evidently perturbed him, because he tapped his pencil on the desk at an increasingly rapid rate. In truth, Larissa was devastated to have been caught. The knot in her stomach felt like a tumor, and she couldn't wait to get home, crawl into bed, and curl up into a ball. Maybe even cry. But for the moment, she had to keep her game face on.

"Personally, I find this disturbing," the middle-aged assistant principal continued. "Really disturbing. Perhaps I should recommend a psychiatric evaluation."

Disturbing? In what kind of special bubble does this man live? A snicker unintentionally escaped her lips, causing Mr. Miller's eyebrows to arch as if someone had just cut in front of him in line at Starbucks. After a beat, he leaned back in his chair. "I reviewed your file, Larissa, and I know you weren't always like this. What's going on?"

Walter Miller really wasn't a bad guy, but of course the students all made fun of him regardless. And although no one would label him as unattractive, the pronounced wrinkles on his forehead and those tired, sagging eyes betrayed a state of perpetual consternation. He would lurk around campus all solemn and severe, but when speaking with him one on one, you could tell he clearly wanted to be liked. Except when you were in trouble. Then he was like a shark sniffing blood in the water.

"Was it your feces?"

Larissa began to feel sorry for old Mr. Miller, given he was trying so earnestly to get to the bottom of things. Life surely amounted to no bowl of cherries for him either. If so, he certainly wouldn't be wiling his time away in this cement prison known as Westlake High. So for better or worse, the adolescent finally met his gaze. "You're just dying to know, aren't you?"

He leaned forward abruptly in his chair. "Let me give you some advice, Larissa. The more you talk, the better. Insolence is only going to make matters worse. Like I said, expulsion is not off the table."

"No, it wasn't my feces. Hope you're not too disappointed. Can I go now?"

"How are things at home?"

"Fantastic. Can I go?"

"Larissa, what's going on between you and Christy? What were you trying to tell her by dumping... manure in her locker?"

Larissa gave Mr. Miller the once-over, and for dramatic effect, adjusted herself in her seat. "You know, you look like you've lost some weight," she said. "Have you been working out?"

"Don't change the subject on me." Mr. Miller was clearly familiar with this type of evasion strategy.

"I like the new haircut too. Shorter definitely makes you look younger. Are you trying to make a good impression on the new men's volleyball coach? Or is it that foxy male secretary? What's his name?"

"My personal life is..."

"None of my business, right?"

Mr. Miller took a deep sigh and shook his head. "We have a psychiatric social worker affiliated with the district who could do an evaluation," he said. The administrator glanced at the student's open file on his desk, probably for dramatic effect as well. "You know, I do have reason to suspect there could be a mental health issue at hand. I believe you know what I'm talking about. Now, I'm only going to ask you one more time. Why did you..."

"She screwed my boyfriend without a condom. There, are you happy now? Christy Carmichael is a boyfriend-stealing skank. Her vaginal cooties are spreading through campus faster than last year's outbreak of crabs. But does she get called into the office? No. Does she get expelled? No. Does she get a psychiatric evaluation? Of course not."

Walter nodded blankly and jotted a few scribbles on his note pad. He then tore off a sheet and offered it to Larissa. "Suspended for the remainder of the week," he blurted. "I'll set up an appointment for you with the school counselor when you return on Monday."

Larissa stood and snatched the paper, relieved the charade was finally over. "Have a fabulous day," she said. "And I mean it; the haircut looks fierce. Meow."

Twenty minutes later, Gary Locke escorted his daughter through the double doors of Westlake High, into the drizzly Northern California air. Several of Larissa's colleagues clapped and cheered during the parking lot processional, which made her feel like a bit of a star. Gary sensed she welcomed the attention, so he gripped even tighter onto her arm and picked up the pace. Once in the car and on their way home, Larissa turned her shoulders to face the window and watched the passing scenery, just as she had done a thousand times before.

"Larissa Abagail Locke," her father began.

"Here we go," she muttered just loud enough to be heard.

"Larissa Abagail Locke. That's what I'm going to name the ulcer that's burning a hole in the pit of my stomach."

Larissa didn't know what to say to this, so she just cleared her throat, trying to remain focused on the blur of the passing neighborhood. "Do you have anything to say for yourself?" her father continued, "Anything at all?"

Turning to face him, she offered, "Hey, didn't you

check your calendar? Today is national Chillax Day."

Gary shifted his focus back and forth between his daughter and the residential street. "What on God's green earth has gotten into you?"

Grounded for a week amounted to a fairly light punishment, Larissa thought later as she unfastened her seat belt and lugged her backpack up the driveway home. After an awkward dinner with her father and brother, the knot still churned in her stomach, so she spent the evening in her room collecting mementos of her and her ex, Lance, placing them in a pile on her desk. Finally, at last, as the room drew somber with fading light, Larissa curled up into a ball on top of her bed and didn't speak to anyone else for the rest of the night.

That night Larissa had a dream. It seemed oddly familiar, as if she had experienced this dream at least once before. Her eyelids parted, and she saw the room glowing bright with amber light. Too bright to think clearly. She was laying in bed with the covers removed. Four middle-aged men stood before her wearing dull brownish-grey clothing and a pasty complexion.

Larissa tried to stand, but immediately found herself unable to budge. It was how she imagined the feeling of being paralyzed from the neck down. One man, who appeared to be the leader of the others was shining a pink light into her eyes, and two of the other men exchanged remarks in a bizarre foreign language.

This leader, who had an inch-long scar on his forehead, retracted the light. "Sorry to wake you," he said. "We'll give you a little something to help you go back to sleep."

"Why can't I move?" Larissa asked in a panic.

"It's only temporary," replied the stoic man. "Nothing to get upset about. We have a medical expert with us to take good care of you."

The man turned away to bark orders at a second figure, an older man with sunspots and white hair, who immediately brandished a thick, fleshy tube. This medical expert slid the tube into the teen's left nostril, making her wince in discomfort. "I don't want to go back to sleep," Larissa screamed. "Leave me alone!"

"Just try to relax," the medicine man replied in a reassuring tone.

"Do not get your panties in a bunch," said a third figure, approaching Larissa's side and resting his hand on her arm. Shorter and heavier with curly locks, he turned to his colleagues to explain. "This is a colloquial expression. A derivative of the British version, 'don't get your knickers in a twist.' It's used in jest to imply that a female's overexaggerated response may twist her undergarments into an unbearable position."

The medical expert nodded and ran his clammy fingers down Larissa's throat to check her pulse, and then turning her head to the side, looked inside her ear. He spoke to the others in their abrasive language.

"I don't need an evaluation," Larissa said.

"It will be completely painless," the man with the scar asserted. "You'll see." Larissa finally got a clear look at the fourth figure. He was slightly taller and paler than the others. There remained very little hair on his head, but his eyes were deep, dark, and frightening. Expressionless, he seemed to look straight through to her soul.

CHAPTER 2

"Larissa!?" For the third time Gary Locke yelled his daughter's name, and given no response, he resorted to pounding on the bedroom door. "Larissa!"

Larissa just couldn't manage to wrench herself out of bed. It felt as if her limbs were useless objects resting by her side. They couldn't take any direction from her brain, even if her brain had any interest in ordering them out of bed.

Gary turned the doorknob and burst inside. Storming over to the window, he pushed aside the curtains, flooding the room in blinding light. "Up and at 'em," he said pulling back her Pink Floyd comforter.

His daughter's body still wouldn't budge, but her eyelids managed to squint in his direction.

"You're mean," she said.

"Just because you're not going to school today doesn't mean you're sleeping 'til noon. Up and at 'em."

Larissa groaned, feeling her extremities slowly return to life. "Five more minutes."

"Negative." Gary glanced at his wrist watch. "It's trash time. Garbage truck's gonna be here any minute." Larissa closed her eyes again, at which point her father yanked the pillow out from underneath her head. "Now! There's a list of chores for you on the fridge. I expect them done by the time I get home."

With what felt like epic strength, Larissa pushed herself up to a seated position. Gary looked her over, and apparently satisfied she had returned to the realm of the living, headed for the door. "And no TV," he blurted before slamming it shut behind him.

Larissa poured herself a full mug of black coffee, took a bitter sip, and read the chore list on the fridge: take out trash, vacuum, wash dishes, rake leaves. She worked her tail off throughout the morning knocking these items off the list, knowing that the quicker she finished, the quicker she could commence 'The Ritual.' Larissa honestly couldn't remember ever feeling so groggy, so she continually refilled her coffee mug as the day progressed until everything was crossed off her list and the coffee pot was dry.

Then, gathering a few pics of her and Lance from a Six Flags photo booth, her ex's Ramones T-shirt, and a fluffy penguin he won for her at the county fair; Larissa placed these items on the barbecue grill in the backyard. Oh, Lance, she thought, why such a chode? He was a guy that first caught her eye four years ago in junior high. Although not a jock, he was naturally very well-proportioned. Good genes. Larissa was captivated by the swirl of sandy brown hair which hung in front of his ocean blue eyes, and yet bitterly resented the fact that anyone could send her senses reeling to such a degree. And when he put his hands on her... "Stop it, Larissa," she said to herself. "Snap out of it or this ritual is never going to get off the ground."

While dousing the mementos with lighter fluid, Larissa noticed Mrs. Sumi, the nosy next-door neighbor to the south, watering the geraniums on her porch. Mrs. Sumi shot the teen her signature look of disapproval, the one Larissa had witnessed time and time again; and when Larissa extracted a box of matches from her pocket, Mrs. Sumi wrinkled her nose. Larissa merely acted as though her neighbor didn't exist, and with a brisk flick of the wrist, set the items ablaze. The young girl remained under the gloomy skies until the last flicker of flames fizzled out and nothing remained on the barbecue but floating ash. Looking over, she saw Mrs. Sumi had finally retreated inside.

Later, when lugging a bag of leaves to the trash bin in the street, Larissa caught sight of Brittany Welles in her lemon lime cheerleading outfit waltzing home from school. Her peppy sixteen year-old neighbor to the north moved onto the block when Larissa was ten years-old. At that time, the two played in the same circles. But puberty changes everything, and once in middle school, the two girls flocked in distinctly different directions.

"So, Larissa," Brittany began as she sidled up to the curb where Larissa dumped the dried leaves, "everybody wants to know, where'd you get the poop from?"

Larissa coolly turned her back to her. "I have my resources."

"I've gotta hand it to you," Brittany continued. "You sure know how to make a statement."

Apparently some people can't take a hint, Larissa thought, as she continued to disregard her neighbor and wrap up the chore.

After a bit of silence, the cheerleader added, "Well, on behalf of the female population at Westlake High, I want to say thank you. Christy Carmichael's a dirty slut who finally got a taste of what's coming to her. You're apparently not the only one who's been burned."

Taken off guard, Larissa turned to face her. "Who else got burned?"

Brittany's cell phone rang, and she reached into the bowels of her purse to retrieve it. "Sometimes I just hate having to keep a secret," she replied. "Anyway, enjoy your vacation," she said as she answered her phone and bounced on home.

Reclining in bed with a sketch pad on her lap, Larissa gripped a charcoal pencil in one hand and her cell phone in the other. At her pencil point lay the self-portrait assigned by her art teacher. "So, it's really not like a vacation after all," Larissa observed into the phone while making faint pencil strokes on the pad. "My dad picks up my homework after work every day."

"That blows," replied Melissa on the other end of the line. "I guess if it was a riot, though, everyone would be getting suspended, right?"

Larissa erased a few marks on the paper. Melissa was her friend tried and true, a close companion since the second grade. The two shared a dark and quirky sense of humor that left some people perplexed and others even slightly disturbed. Their peculiar friendship truly took off during the holiday season four years earlier, when she and Melissa kidnapped an electric Santa Claus from the most obnoxiously decorated yard in the neighborhood. They left behind a sinister ransom note, but then realizing its collection would prove too dangerous, they decided to find Santa a new home. Placing Santa at the front door of her surly history teacher's house, Larissa rang the bell, and the two BFFs bolted down the street to the park. Despite the brisk December air, the two laughed on the swing set for twenty minutes that night until Larissa thought she was going to pee her pants.

"Now I have to do this self-portrait for art class," Larissa continued into the phone. "It seems like no matter what I do, I always end up looking pissed off." She glanced across the room to study her reflection in the dresser mirror, then made a few strokes on the pad.

"Well, I should probably let you know something," Melissa said, stumbling over her words. "I'm gonna see if I can switch to Spanish."

"Why Spanish?"

"If I switch to Spanish, I'll have first period lunch; which means I'll get to eat with Anthony." Larissa gasped. Although she tolerated Melissa's James Dean wannabe boyfriend Anthony, the truth was that he had recently robbed Larissa of a lot of precious time with her best friend.

"Don't! Who will I eat with?" Larissa pleaded.

"Bethany and Joanna."

"Vomit. We've always had lunch together."

"I know," Melissa conceded. "But this is Anthony's last year, and we want to spend as much time together as possible."

"But what if you break up?" Larissa suggested, carefully testing the waters. "Not that that's what I'm hoping for. But then you will have switched for nothing. Don't do it."

Melissa sighed. "Well, I'll think about it."

"Girl, you da bomb." Larissa was temporarily relieved, but realized storm clouds could soon darken the horizon. She could think of nothing more terrifying than being left alone to fend for oneself in the cut-throat social landscape of second period lunch.

"By the way, you'd better watch your back when you come back 'cause Christy's apparently beyond furious," Melissa continued.

"I think I can hold my own."

"Well listen, I better go call Anthony before dinner."

"Of course."

"Later."

Larissa dropped the phone and took a look at her portrait. With the facial features noticeably disproportionate and the vacant expression in the eyes, the figure in the drawing looked like a mad woman. She tore the paper from the pad, crumpled it up, and tossed it in the trash can next to a handful of other rejected portraits. Then, taking another look at herself in the mirror, she began again on a fresh slice.

The scene from a retro sci-fi flick playing on TV reminded Larissa of her dream the night before. The nightmare had completely escaped her mind, but once the deadpan aliens emerged from their flying saucer, she couldn't help but think of the four creepy men that stood at the side of her bed. Naturally, Larissa had heard stories of alien visitation, and her dream did in fact seem reminiscent of some of those tales. She had never thought seriously about their legitimacy, but watching the film brought the mysterious phenomenon to the forefront of her mind. The creatures on TV seemed goofy with their oblong skulls and bug-like eyes, and so their appearance held no resemblance to the men in her dream.

From behind the sofa came the occasional racket

of her younger brother, Carter, putting golf balls into a teacup. "Righteous," the fourteen year-old cheered as he sank a hole-in-one.

"Dinner time," her father yelled from the kitchen. Larissa lingered for a moment, enraptured by the inexpressive nature of the latex creatures on TV before venturing into the kitchen. A short time later, the three ate their meals silently around the table.

"I was looking through your trig homework earlier," Gary said, breaking the ice. "If you need any help with your functions, remember I used to be quite a math ace in high school."

"It's all right," Larissa replied. "I've got it."

"Well, actually I'm not so sure you do. C plus on your last quiz, that's hardly stellar." Larissa groaned and toyed with her gnocchi. The last thing she wanted was a lecture from her father on the minutiae of trigonometry. They had danced this dance a million times over in algebra. Gary would attempt to prove his mathematical genius while making Larissa feel like a complete dumb ass. She would then plead to be left alone, at which point he would label her ungrateful for rejecting the superior knowledge he was willing to so graciously impart.

While Larissa remained unresponsive, Gary and Carter exchanged an uncomfortable glance. Fearing another argument brewing, Carter cleared his throat. "So Sin(x) walks into a bar and the bartender says, 'Sorry, we don't cater functions,'" he said.

Another awkward silence ensued. Gary turned again to his daughter, "So, what do you say?"

"Dad..." Larissa began with an exasperation-infused voice, but then quickly changed her tone. "Oh, never mind."

"What?"

"You don't wanna hear it."

Her father reflected for a moment, then resumed eating. "Ya know, that's all right. They're your functions, not mine. Have fun with them." He sulked and Larissa was secretly relieved to have averted another incident. Gary then turned his attention to Carter. "So, you working this weekend?"

"I don't know, it's supposed to rain on Sunday. Tournament will probably get kicked back a week."

Gary nodded. Carter had been working as a caddy at the local golf club for the past year. His father took great pride in his son for taking on the additional responsibility and showing the initiative to earn some money at such a young age.

"Hey, if it rains, do you think we could go see Mom?" Carter asked. The boy and his sister exchanged a tentative look. The father paused, fork in midair.

"Yeah," Gary said after a moment. "You know, I think that would be all right. I'll call the hospital and let them know we may be coming."

Larissa smiled and finished her meal. After two months of no contact, a visit was certainly in order.

When Larissa opened her eyes later that night, she found herself again paralyzed in bed, the room bathed in amber light. The four pale men encircled her, the leader of whom produced a large, black needle resembling a talon.

"You're awake," he said. "Just a pinch." The scarred man passed the needle to his associate with the sunspots, who carefully inserted the needle into Larissa's arm. She bit her lip in pain.

"Stop. Just stop," Larissa pleaded, unable to prevent tears from forming.

The examiners ignored her and conversed in their sharp alien tongue. The leader then turned to the teen with false affection, "Larissa, we're going to give you something to calm your nerves." He motioned to the medical authority, who inserted the fleshy tube into her nostril.

"What do you want from me?" she sobbed.

"Take a few deep breaths," said the medical expert. "You won't even know we're here."

"I don't want you here," Larissa retorted.

The third figure with curly locks smiled down at her in a way which she found revolting. He softly sang, "Baa, baa, black sheep, Have you any wool? Yes, sir, yes, sir, Three bags full." The last thing Larissa perceived was the fourth figure, the one with the dark eyes, standing in the corner gazing into her eyes, expressionless.

CHAPTER 3

Although the alarm clock clamored into her right ear, Larissa remained buried in the pillow. Carter rushed in to kill the noise. "Bust a move," he said, shutting off the alarm, plopping down on the bed, and waiting for his sister to respond.

"I can't get up," she finally uttered.

"You need a bean?"

Larissa nodded. Carter opened her night stand drawer and retrieved a stash of chocolate covered espresso beans. His sister rolled over and parted her chapped lips, then Carter dumped five beans in her mouth and took a few for himself.

"Is it true that if you think you're going crazy," Larissa wondered aloud, "then you're really not?" Carter studied her without saying anything for a while.

"How the hell would I know?" he said at last before dropping the pack of beans on the bed and splitting.

Nearly a half-hour later, the groggy teen grabbed the chore list from the refrigerator: dusting, laundry, and windows. She robotically took care of these chores as quickly as she could, because again, Larissa had her own business to attend to.

While upstairs cleaning the vanity mirror in her bathroom, Larissa detected a tiny round scar on her right arm. She stopped wiping, frozen stiff. Was this for real? A coincidence, maybe? The image of the curved talon from the dream resurfaced in her mind's eye. She inspected the tender, pink wound, which was slightly larger than a mosquito bite. Her memory of the dream remained fuzzy, but she swore the needle had been inserted into her right arm. Could it just be an insect bite? It was slightly swollen, but lacking the itching sensation of a mosquito bite. And mosquitoes weren't usually found buzzing around in Northern California in mid-January.

Larissa sat down on the side of the tub holding her arm and mulling over the events she could recall from her dreams the past two nights. Only bits and pieces came back. Surely, she thought, no one could come into the house without waking her father or Carter. But what if someone came in through the window? Larissa remembered the sci-fi flick she saw on TV the night before and recollected hearing stories about alien abduction. Have I been probed, she wondered?

If so, isn't the victim supposed to be beamed up to the spaceship for examination? That's how the story goes, anyway.

Later, with the credenza dusted and laundry folded, Larissa fired up the Internet. She typed the words 'alien abduction' into a search engine and perused the nine million results. Her first stop was an on-line encyclopedia, which characterized alien abduction as "intricate physical procedures performed by nonhuman entities." According to the author, the phenomena remained discounted by the scientific community due to the lack of any objective physical evidence. That said, the page offered insight into what could lead to such an 'experience,' such as sleep paralysis or false memory syndrome.

Clicking on a recent video that appeared intriguing, she began watching an on-line documentary made up of alien abduction survivors describing their encounters. It began with a famous couple from the 1960's abducted on a New Hampshire roadside one evening. Listening to their hypnosis tapes, Larissa could genuinely sense their pain and horror as they recounted how a dwarfish alien beamed them into its spacecraft and inserted a long needle into their navels.

Most of the interviewees were abducted roadside, but there were a few who claimed to have been taken from their bedrooms. These stories had an eerily familiar ring to them. "When I woke up, I couldn't move," one woman said. Her face remained in shadow to conceal her identity. "And then I saw one of them standing at the foot of my bed. 'Don't be afraid,' it said. 'We're not going to harm you. We're just going to do some tests."' The reenactment footage included a goofy CGI alien tiptoeing through the unfortunate woman's cluttered room. Larissa instinctively hit pause, freezing the extraterrestrial in mid-creep. He looked nothing like the men from her nightmare, she noted. All the abductees described 'greys,' or short men with long appendages and bulging black eyes. Was it possible that aliens now had the power to alter their appearance and walk among us as fellow humans? Don't get yourself all worked up, Larissa reassured herself. It's just a stupid dream.

Hitting play again, she watched an abduction specialist elaborate. "Almost all abduction scenarios take place at night," she began. "And the majority of abductees are women. These abductees often find themselves waking up in the middle of the night surrounded by amber light." Amber light, Larissa thought, check. "The paralysis makes it impossible for abductees to defend themselves, refuse the experiments, or to escape." Paralysis, check. "Eighty-eight percent of abductees are taken on more than one occasion, and a number of them are taken periodically over the span of many years." More than once, check. "After these experiences, abductees typically suffer from extreme fatigue, nausea, and disorientation." Fatigue, uber check.

"I saw one of them alongside my bed," another female abductee recounted on the verge of tears. "I couldn't move. I felt an overwhelming sense of terror. The creature had a long needle and stuck it into my neck."

Larissa took another sip of coffee. Over the reenactment footage, a psychologist elaborated, "There is frequently a sexual element to these abduction experiences. In a few instances, abductees even report mating with extra-terrestrials."

Larissa shuddered at the thought of those four older men having free reign over her unconscious body, and then the doorbell rang. Heading to the window, she peered outside and saw Lance at the front door, hands in his pockets and kicking the doormat. He peeked inside the downstairs window and rang the doorbell again. "Ass drizzle," Larissa muttered to herself from above.

After two tedious minutes, Lance finally split, and she returned to her computer to select another video. Over the next hour, Larissa listened to story after story. Her overall impression was that, regardless of whatever actually happened to these individuals, the abductees were not lying. But could they all be crazy?

A male abductee, whose face remained obscured in shadow, gave a solemn interview. "I'm not thrilled to have been chosen," he said. "And I regret telling people about it. I've lost a lot of good friends over this. Nobody likes to be thought of as a lunatic. And once people see you in that light, they don't ever go back."

With the garage door propped open and iTunes playing in the background, Larissa sat on a cement block flipping through a tattoo magazine while her brother, Carter, rebuilt the engine to his golf cart.

"Mother of Mary," he said.

"What?" Larissa inquired.

"I'm gonna need a new piston. This rod journal's scratched like a mofo."

"Maybe Santa will be good to you this year."

"I don't wanna wait 'til Christmas," he said. "You think Santa'll give me an advance?"

His sister smirked. "How's your credit?" Larissa knew very well that Carter's credit was solid. He avoided trouble like the plague. Carter grabbed a screwdriver and resumed his work.

"So how fast is that hunk-o-junk gonna go anyway?" she wondered while checking out pics of the latest body art.

"Sixty, if all goes well."

"You're gonna be such a chick magnet in about two years."

"You're saying I'm not one already?"

At that point Larissa performed her signature teenage eye roll and flipped the page. "Hey, do you believe in UFOs?" she asked after a moment.

"Why? You drop acid again?"

"Why don't you believe me when I say that was a one-time thing?"

"Why do you want to know?" Carter asked with a trace of intrigue in his voice. He proceeded to install a face plate onto the motor casing.

"Just saw something on the Internet," she replied. "No big whoop."

Carter sighed and put down his wrench. "The closest planet capable of sustaining life is thousands of light years away. So, by the time ET left home, he would be over a thousand years-old by the time he got here. That is, if he was traveling at light speed. What do you think?"

Larissa nodded and turned the page. A spider must've bitten my arm in the night, she told herself. Her subconscious had spun the incident into a wild story of alien visitors in order to cope with a completely common insect bite. There were certainly no aliens visiting Planet Earth, she resolved. How could there be?

The members of the Locke family found themselves on the road early Sunday morning, the rain pounding like a barrage of bullets onto the windshield. Gary drove while Carter passed the time on his iPad playing a video game in the passenger seat. In the back, Larissa gazed out the window, lost in thought. Two days had elapsed since her last 'nightmare,' and after two nights of solid rest, she was almost feeling herself again. In spite of the rain, her father was in a noticeably positive mood. "I spy with my eye something that starts with the letter R," he said.

Silence followed. I'm gonna pretend I didn't just hear that, Larissa thought to herself.

"Anyone?" her father continued.

"Range Rover," Carter offered in a poor attempt to

disguise his resentment at the momentary distraction.

"Nope," replied Gary. Silence ensued. "Anyone else?"

Damn, Larissa thought. He just doesn't know when to give up. "Rain," she said at last.

"Good guess, but no." Silence. "Rearview mirror," Gary finally explained.

"Wow," said Carter with more attitude than Larissa had seen from him in a while. "That's a great one, Dad."

The Chrysler drove past the suburbs and into the rural countryside. "Dad?" Carter asked.

"Yep?"

"What's she going to be like?"

Gary took a beat to mull this over. "Well, you know she's still your mom."

"Is she gonna be all depressed and stuff?" Carter asked.

"Um... yeah. It takes a while to get better. And being in the hospital isn't any fun. She'd rather be home with you kids." Carter nodded. "But keep in mind," the father continued. "She could be very tired. We need to take it easy on your mom today." Gary looked directly at his daughter through the rearview mirror. "Okay, pumpkin?"

"Yeah. Of course," Larissa responded indignantly.

The Chrysler pulled into the sprawling parking lot of the Winchester Hospital for Mental Health. Through the car window, Larissa glanced up at the contemporary stucco and brick edifice. Surprisingly quaint, not what she had expected.

Stepping through the sliding glass doors of the marble lobby, Larissa's mind immediately flashed back six years to the night they rushed Carter to the emergency room with an intense pain in his abdomen. Her mother and father were anxious like she had never seen before. Once they discovered Carter suffered from a run-of-the-mill appendicitis, they breathed a sigh of relief. That said, the cold lobby reminded Larissa of the look of excruciating pain on Carter's face and the subsequent hours of pacing during the operation. "Why don't you two sit down for a minute?" Gary said, then he headed to the reception desk. Carter and his sister took a seat and perused the rumpled magazines on the table. They could both sense each other's excitement and apprehension.

After Gary signed in, the young brunette at the reception took a second look at his name. "Oh, yeah," she said. "We tried reaching you this morning." She then noticed Larissa and Carter in the sitting area. "You wanna step inside for a second?" Gary nodded, and the receptionist hit a buzzer that unlocked the two thick doors with smoked glass panes leading inside.

"So what are you getting Mom for her birthday?" Carter asked, watching his father disappear through the double doors.

"I don't know," Larissa answered. "Probably a book or something. What about you?"

"Probably a book."

Larissa pondered life beyond those double doors with the frosted glass. She thought about madness and wondered if she would someday find herself its victim. After two minutes, their father reemerged from inside and approached his children. As they stood, Larissa noticed that his eyes were red and watery.

"I'm afraid Mom's not feeling so good today," Gary said. "The doctors say it's in her best interest if we come back another day. So, let's get back in the car and head on home, okay? Maybe we can stop at that ice cream place on the way."

Carter and his sister nodded, unsure of what to say. After coming all this way, they now felt confused and disappointed. Later, the three of them rode home in silence while spooning ice cream into their unhappy faces.

Dressed for bed, Larissa cleaned her teeth with a tattered brush. Was her mom gravely ill? What had the nurse told her father, and why wasn't he giving her the whole story? He must've known something and was holding back. Larissa felt conflicted; on one hand she wanted more info, and yet on the flip side, she feared learning the truth. Was her mother beyond help? Was she destined to spend the remainder of her life caged up in a mental institution? And what did that mean for Larissa? The adolescent recollected overhearing a news segment on TV recently about the genetic predisposition of mental illness.

After spitting, Larissa looked to the wound on her arm, but found it completely healed. You couldn't tell it had even been there at all. Then, something in the mirror caught her eye. She noticed a couple of golfing magazines scattered across the floor near the commode. Carter had clearly been reading them while on the pot. The cover of one showed the picture of a man who looked eerily familiar. In fact, he looked just like Larissa's nocturnal visitor, forehead scar and all. She stowed her toothbrush and grabbed the magazine. The cover displayed an action photo of a golf star swinging a driver in the daytime sun. She dug further into the magazine and found more pictures of the sinister look-alike. Then on the back cover, she found an ad depicting the image of another man from her dreams, the man with sunspots. He was holding up a golf trophy while wearing a smug grin on his face. Larissa nervously tore through the other magazines, finding images of the remaining two visitors. Now she feared more than ever that insanity was beginning to take hold. It felt as though the bathroom walls were starting to close in on her.

Mentally wiped out, Larissa headed for bed, stopping at her window to check the lock. Finding it unlatched, she immediately locked it tight. That's not good, she thought before jumping in bed. How long had it been that way?

Hours later, Larissa opened her eyes to a squint. Again, the paralysis. The piercing amber light. Or was her vision simply distorted? Her mouth was pried open by two long probes, while Sunspots and Scarface inspected the inside of her mouth. Upon noticing her awakened state, they retracted the instruments.

"Fuck you," Larissa said.

Scarface looked to Curly Locks and raised his eyebrows. "A vulgarity," the latter explained. "Difficult to trace the origin."

"You're a stubborn girl who doesn't like to sleep," the leader said while watching his subject tear up. At the edge of the amber light, the fourth figure, Dark Eyes, emitted some screeching sounds, at which point Scarface and Sunspots bitterly spewed a few indecipherable words in his direction. Then, Dark Eyes regarded the girl with an odd expression that resembled concern. Sunspots retrieved a tube from out of nowhere and tried to slide it up her nose, but she evaded him by turning her head to the side. But forcing her head down, he succeeded in his second attempt to insert the tube into her nostril.

"No! Stop it!" Larissa screamed.

"No point in making a fuss," replied Sunspots.

Her eyes fell on Curly Locks. He held a clear fleshy bag in his hand, a translucent sac with purple veins running through it. The bag quivered and then slowly filled with blood. What on earth? But soon enough, she discovered the answer. Her eyes followed a tube running from the twitching bag which led to a needle inserted into her arm.

"We just gave you something to make you sleepy," said Scarface. "Otherwise, you're doing really fantastic, Larissa." Dark Eyes made some abrasive remarks, and then Sunspots checked her pulse. Curly Locks examined the blood-filled bag, and once completely full, Sunspots carefully removed the needle from her arm. Then the needle, seeming to have a life of its own, retracted itself underneath the medical expert's pale grey coat.

Larissa opened her mouth to scream, but nothing would come out. Scarface and Sunspots swapped a concerned look.

Larissa woke up gasping, alone in her dark room. It took a few minutes to catch her breath and calm down before getting out of bed and hurrying to the window. There, she found it locked as before.

So this is what it's like to go crazy, Larissa thought. The melancholy double doors of Winchester Mental Hospital may well be opening for her in the near future, and the vision made her heart sink.

With heavy breath, Larissa went to the bathroom, turned on the faucet, and took a drink of water. Out of the corner of her eye, she swore she saw something move. Something thin and swift. She looked over in the direction of the toilet to discover a long pink tentacle, slithering into the porcelain bowl and vanishing from sight.

The girl cautiously approached the toilet and peered inside. There was nothing there. Then two seconds later, she threw up the entire contents of her TV dinner inside.

CHAPTER 4

Normally, Larissa and her father didn't talk much on the way to school. But the following day, the pair didn't speak so much as a two words to one another. He assumed she was pouting over some overblown teenage melodrama. Larissa just couldn't think of anything to say.

When they arrived at Westlake High, the bell had already rung and the students were flocking to class. Gary pulled up alongside the curb, and his daughter hopped out. "I will, thank you," her father said, clearly frustrated. "You have a nice day too." Larissa ignored him and headed to class.

The mass of students took no notice of her as she entered the building. Larissa pulled open her squeaky locker door and grabbed the textbooks needed for morning class, just as Melissa strolled up alongside and opened her own locker, strategically located alongside her friend's.

"You're back," Melissa said. "Bet you missed us, huh?"

"Feels like I never left," Larissa replied. "Unfortunately."

Melissa smirked and closed her locker door. "See you at lunch, gangsta." As Melissa disappeared, Larissa crammed her Government book inside the locker and shut the door.

"Hey, Christy," she heard a voice say from down the hall. Larissa froze, realizing the inevitable moment of confrontation had arrived. She gained her composure and turned to leave, stopping short just as Christy Carmichael and two of her cronies almost collided with her. Upon noticing Larissa, Christy gave her the stare down and thrust her twiggy middle finger in Larissa's face.

"Hi, stinky," Larissa uttered calmly.

"You think you're a bad ass?" Christy asked. Larissa shrugged in reply. "You think you're tough? We'll have to see about that." After a prolonged moment, Christy finally passed by and Larissa moseyed off to Trig.

Larissa remained in an absolute daze during class, reflecting back at what she had seen in the bathroom the night before. She now was seriously contemplating the idea that she may be delusional. Bizarre dreams were one thing, but visions while awake amounted to another situation entirely. Was her mom also suffering from delusions? Was this a hereditary gene passed from mother to child? Was it only going to get worse as time progressed? The thought sank Larissa into a deep depression. When Mr. Berg called on her for an answer, she asked politely if he could call on someone else.

"Great attitude, Larissa," he remarked.

"I'm not trying to give you attitude," she replied. "I'm just not feeling that well."

"If you're sick, then go see the nurse."

Later in fourth period, twenty high schoolers sat in Mrs. Morales' art class at work tables in front of a collection of supplies: small planks of wood, wire, and paper mâché. As usual, Mrs. Morales gave instruction while seated on top of her steel desk situated at the head of the classroom. "As you've probably guessed," she said, "today we're moving into another dimension. Our next project is going to be three dimensional. You're going to take what you have in front of you and create a sculpture. Your inspiration is this: someone whom you see at school. Doesn't need to be a specific person. Think generally."

The students gradually began to twist wire into human shapes. Larissa reluctantly toyed with the material, still unsure of what concept to settle on. Next to her sat perky Brittany Welles, who again donned her polyester lemon lime cheerleader outfit.

Mrs. Morales paced up and down the aisles. "First, obviously, you're going to want to work out the frame," she said. "The stronger, more solid structure the better." Examining everyone's progress, Mrs. Morales stopped alongside Brittany. "And what have you decided on?"

"A cheerleader," replied Brittany.

"Staying close to home, I see. You should have an interesting perspective." Brittany constructed a circular object with a piece of wire. "What's this?" Mrs. Morales asked.

"A toilet. She's bulimic." Brittany looked to Larissa, and the two couldn't help but share a smile.

The teacher patted Brittany on the shoulder. "You're adorable," she said while continuing down the aisle.

The bell eventually rang and everyone filed into the hallway. Brittany and Larissa left class side by side. "I'm having a couple friends over for a slumber party on Saturday night," Brittany said. "You should come." Larissa didn't respond immediately. "That is, if you're not grounded," the cheerleader added.

"Are you kidding?" Larissa replied. "My dad would love it. He thinks you'd be a great influence on me."

"Then come on over."

"A slumber party? Isn't that sorta middle school?"

Brittany shrugged. "We have a good time."

"I'll think about it."

"Okay. See ya."

Larissa left to go meet Melissa for lunch. Why on earth would Brittany invite her to a slumber party? Especially after four years of barely saying one word to her. Surely, there had to be an ulterior motive.

After lunch, Larissa set foot in Ms. Patterson's office, where the youngish guidance counselor sipped a mocha while checking her e-mail. Her clothes were fashionable for a woman nearing thirty, although not expensive. Her hair was layered in a way as if to say, "I'm all business from nine to five, but after hours... watch out."

"Hi, sweetheart," Ms. Patterson said, noticing Larissa sulk in the door frame. "Grab a seat." The teen meandered over to the plastic chair and plopped down. "You're Larissa, right?"

Larissa nodded, wanting to offer as little to the experience as possible. After all, in her mind this was a private matter, and there was really nothing to discuss.

"Great. I'm Ms. Patterson. Mr. Miller wanted us to spend a few sessions together." The counselor opened a manila file folder with Larissa's name on it and took out a note pad. "Glad to be back at school?"

Larissa shrugged.

"Right. So, here's a question for you right off the bat. Are you interested in going to college?"

"Sure," Larissa offered. "Why not?" In truth, she felt indifferent about college. Her older cousin Mary worked as a waitress and once said that all college ever did was make her more knowledgeable than her asshole manager at Denny's. That said, Larissa figured that if she was doomed to wait tables at Denny's for the rest of her life, she might as well delay it for four years by going to college.

41

"You know, high school stress is one thing," Ms. Patterson said, "but when you go to college, it's a whole different ball game. You've got a more intense academic environment, a whole new social scene to navigate, new emotional stresses. Do you think you're capable of handling all of that?"

Larissa ruminated for a second. "I guess. There's only one way to find out."

Ms. Patterson nodded. "Are you happy with what you did to Christy's locker?"

"I...I don't know."

"What do you think you gained from that?"

"I was really pissed," Larissa said, reluctantly showing some fervor.

"And rightfully so. Christy hurt you. So, you got revenge. How does that feel?"

"It feels fine."

"Fine? Tell me, if you could go back and do it all over again, would you do anything differently? Or are you happy with how this all panned out?"

"Well..." Larissa paused and bit her lip. How happy was she with how things transpired? In truth, she had never really stopped to think about it.

Ms. Patterson waited patiently for a response. "There's no right or wrong answer," she said. "Just think about it. Maybe next time you can tell me. I'm trying to gauge whether or not you feel your actions were worth the consequences. If you do, then you do. But I think this is a very important question for you to answer."

Larissa sighed. Clearly, she had not been prepared for this woman to take her job so seriously.

That night, Larissa attempted to finish her home-work in bed, but just couldn't concentrate. Without warning, her father appeared at the door. "Lights out."

"I'll be done in five minutes," she said.

"Five minutes, then." Gary left his daughter to her Government essay, which she typed laboriously into her laptop. Her phone dinged, and Larissa noticed a Snapchat message from Lance-a-lot which read, "For-give me?" Although tempted to block Lance from all social media outlets, she had opted for the moment to keep him as a "friend" in the event she ever wished to spy on his latest hijinks. But for right now, she ignored the message and kept typing.

After trudging through her essay on checks and balances, Larissa shut down and stowed the laptop on her desk. Then, peering out the bedroom door, she saw her father's light go out at the other end of the hall.

Larissa pulled a spool of thread from her sewing box and tied it to one end of a skateboard, which had been sitting neglected in the closet for some time. She then ripped the comforter off her bed, and tossed it, along with a pillow into the hallway. Exiting her room, Larissa carefully propped the skateboard against the inside of the door, so that if her door were to open during the night, the skateboard would roll.

Closing the door behind her, she tiptoed down the

hallway. In one hand she held the pillow and comforter, and in the other hand the spool, which trailed the thread behind her as she went.

Heading down the stairs, Larissa carefully laid the thread along the banister. She tied the other end of the thread to an antique porcelain bell, which she laid on the table next to the sofa. Then, plopping herself down on the couch, she pulled the comforter over her head and closed her eyes.

Tonight is the night Larissa's going to get some answers, she thought to herself. Dream or no dream, crazy or sane, it's time for Larissa Locke to know what the hell she's dealing with.

CHAPTER 5

The suburbs of Walnut Creek, California seemed more still than usual that night. After tossing and turning on the sofa for two hours, Larissa was on the brink of drifting off to sleep when she perceived a slight ding. It didn't quite register at first. Then the bell by her side dinged again and her eyes flashed open. The bell rang a third time, and this time she sat up, throwing the comforter aside. Rushing to the stairs, she looked up to the second floor and listened. Nothing.

Larissa climbed the steps one by one. Given her history of sneaking out at night more times than she could count, she possessed detailed knowledge of the location of all creaky floorboards. Maneuvering them like land mines, she arrived at the top in silence. Before rounding the corner to her bedroom, she scrunched down and pulled out a make-up mirror from her pocket. Holding the mirror out and to the side, she got a fairly clear view of the hallway.

Her door was ajar. Waiting in the stairwell, Larissa tried to calm her breathing, which had abruptly become rapid and shallow. The bedroom door opened wider, and in a panic, she pulled the mirror back and out of sight. Something or someone was undoubtedly lurking in her room.

After summoning her courage, Larissa extended the mirror out again. What she saw at that moment defied her wildest imagination. A mass was making its way slowly across the hallway floor. It stood about three feet off the ground, held upright by four long spiny appendages. The body of the creature consisted of an oblong grey torso divided into segments, at the end of which protruded what appeared to be its neckless head. Larissa assumed it was the head because of the two antennae held at attention above its pair of opaque black eyes. At least a dozen thin, pink tentacles spilled out of its tail end, almost seeming to have wills of their own. Even from down the hall, the smell of this cricket-like creature was repulsive. Fighting the urge to scream, Larissa retracted the mirror and shut her eyes in an attempt to remove the filthy image from her mind.

Larissa couldn't fathom what she had just seen. After calming her frazzled nerves, she held the mirror up again, just in time to see the creature disappear into Carter's room. A tentacle slithering behind. At once, she felt the impulse to rush to her brother's aid, but hesitated. Without any method of defense, her presence could in fact do them both more harm than good. She thought of dashing to the Sumi house for help, but then reconsidered; doubting they would even open the door for their troubled teenage neighbor. So, she waited.

The clock on the wall ticked three twenty-seven AM. Did this entity slither through the sewer system and up through the toilet? Given its size and shape, she didn't see how that could be feasible. Larissa waited a full hour in anguish. Then came the creaking of Carter's bedroom door. She held out the mirror and peered down the hallway. Scarface, Sunspots, Curly Locks, and Dark Eyes all exited Carter's room, appearing as they had in her dreams. Scarface pointed in Larissa's direction toward the stairwell. She retracted the mirror and silently began to creep down the stairs. Oblivious to her presence; Scarface, Sunspots, Curly Locks, and Dark Eyes all walked past the stairwell and entered her father's bedroom.

Larissa made her way to the foot of the stairs, where she ended up pacing frantically in the kitchen. Could it be that these grotesque sewer creatures were altering their appearance in order to appear human? Noticing the butcher block on the counter, she grabbed a butcher knife and hid inside the pantry. There, she dropped to a fetal position.

A long night passed in the pantry with her mind racing. Her thoughts ricocheted back and forth between worry for her family's safety, and concern for her own questionable sanity. Larissa knew the idea of monsters climbing through the drain and shape-shifting into middle-aged men was preposterous. But if this was the case, where did these creatures originate from, and what were they? In spite of these unanswered questions, some time before dawn, she finally drifted off to sleep.

The distant buzz of dual alarm clocks roused Larissa from her dream. She jolted upright, amazed she had been able to fall asleep at all. When she cracked opened the pantry door, the sunlight streaming into the kitchen momentarily blinded her. Larissa grabbed the butcher knife and nervously proceeded to the stairs, the alarm clock buzz growing louder and louder with each step to the second floor.

At the top of the stairs, Larissa peeked around the corner. Seeing no one, she headed to Carter's room, fearful of what she may discover. There, she found her brother laying face down on top of his covers, completely unconscious. She leaped on the bed and gave him a forceful nudge.

"Wake up!" she yelled. Larissa looked to the alarm clock on his night table and saw it was past nine o'clock. She shut off the alarm, and when she turned Carter over onto his back, he emitted a soft snore. "Carter!" she yelled.

Her brother opened his left eye. "Drop dead," he

finally murmured.

Larissa was ecstatic to hear him speak. "It's after nine," she said. "You're late for school!"

"Don't yank my chain," he retorted.

Larissa stormed out of the room and then re-entered moments later with her stash of chocolate covered espresso beans. She opened Carter's mouth then dumped the entire bag inside. Carter choked. Then glancing to the clock, he noticed the time.

"What happened?"

"You overslept. Now get up!"

Larissa rushed out of the room and down the hall, bursting through her father's door. Despite his alarm clock blaring, Gary was out as well.

"Dad, wake up!" She grabbed the covers and threw them to the side. "Time to get up. You're late!" After no response, she pulled the pillow out from underneath his head.

Gary opened an eye. "Go back to sleep, honey."

"You're late for work." The phone then rang, so Larissa picked up. "Hello?"

"Hi... Larissa?"

"Yeah?"

"This is Jeanie, your dad's secretary."

"Hi."

"Your dad has a meeting at nine thirty today, and he's not here."

"I know," she stammered. "His car wouldn't start."

"Did you call AAA?"

"Yeah, they're fixing the car now. He'll be there in half-an-hour."

"Should I postpone the meeting then?" Suspicion was coming through loud and clear from the other end of the line. "Can I talk to your dad?"

"He can't come to the phone right now," Larissa insisted. "Just postpone the meeting 'til ten thirty. Can you do that?"

"Um... all right. Are you sure everything's okay?"

"Yeah. Everything's fine."

Moments later, the catatonic father took a seat behind the wheel of his Chrysler. Larissa fastened his seat belt and shut the door. She then passed him a mug of coffee through the window.

"Thank you, honey," Gary managed to say. He put the car in gear, and the Chrysler rolled down the driveway.

In the kitchen, Carter was shoveling down spoon-fuls of sugary cereal when his sister burst back inside. "I had the weirdest dream," he offered.

"Get your backpack," she said. "I'm driving you to school."

"You don't have a car."

Larissa crammed her Government textbook into her backpack and snatched a hoodie. "I'll improvise."

Within minutes, the souped-up golf cart came to a screeching halt at the curb of Griffin Middle School. Carter hopped out and ran to class, while Larissa peeled away in haste.

When she pulled into a nearly full parking lot at

Westlake High that morning, all was tranquil and still. The students were inside wrapping up second period. Larissa pulled the golf cart into one of the last remaining spots and dashed out to the sound of the third period bell ringing.

Speaking with the janitor, Mr. Miller observed Larissa's attempt to slip in unnoticed, at which point she offered him a wry shrug. Students filed into the hallway and she soon became engulfed in the swarm. As Melissa retrieved a book from her locker, Larissa approached and opened the one adjacent.

"Hey, what happened?" questioned Melissa. "I was wondering if you were gonna show."

"Lost track of time," she responded.

Melissa smirked as she slammed her locker door. "That's a good one. See you at lunch."

"Later." Larissa hung her hoodie in the locker and swapped a few textbooks.

When she finally slid into her seat for English class, she uttered an audible sigh of relief. For sure she looked like hell, but didn't care. Both Carter and her father had experienced the same encounter last night that she had been victim to before. In her mind, this could only mean one thing—that she wasn't going crazy, and the realization brought a smile to her typically dour face. Then when class started and the teacher's voice droned on, her smile disappeared. She may not be crazy, she realized, but something was crawling out of her toilet at night and wreaking havoc on her and her family. This wasn't exactly awesome either.

CHAPTER 6

Toward the end of third period English, a particularly hoarse female student was reading aloud "The Hollow Men" by T.S. Eliot. "Shape without form, shade without colour," she read robotically, "Paralyzed force, gesture without motion; Those who have crossed With direct eyes, to death's other Kingdom."

The spoken words produced goosebumps on Larissa's arm. A movement in the next aisle over grabbed her attention, and she caught a glimpse of her ex Lance passing a note to a nearby student and then nodding to her.

"Remember us—if at all—not as lost Violent

souls," the hoarse teen continued, "but only As the hollow men. The stuffed men. Eyes I dare not meet in dreams In death's dream kingdom."

The student stealthily laid the note on Larissa's desk. After a moment's contemplation, she took it and folded it into a triangle. Then, holding it upright with one finger, she flicked it with another sending it soaring across the room. The students giggled, and the English teacher looked up from his text, perplexed.

Later, the cafeteria during second period lunch was a combination of long tables, hungry kids, and lots of chatter. Larissa seated herself opposite Melissa and munched on some soggy fries.

"Joanna's been hooking up with this guy who makes fake ID's," Melissa said. "She's gonna get one for you and one for me. Score!"

Larissa didn't respond.

"Hello? Did you hear what I said? Fake ID!"

"Sorry," she said, snapping out of it. "That's dope."

"You're a space cadet today."

"OTR."

"Really? I thought we were on the same cycle."

Larissa shrugged.

"Oh, look," Melissa said softly enough to not be overheard. "Here comes little Ms. Perfect to brighten our day." Brittany Welles sauntered nearby carrying a lunch tray and searching for some companions. She stopped at the next table over to chat with some trendy colleagues. "Perfect hair, perfect teeth, perfect tits," Melissa continued. "Having a perfect conversation about her perfect little life."

"Accumulating votes for Prom Queen, no doubt," Larissa surmised.

Brittany laughed with her friends and proceeded to the next table down, where she found a seat amid Westlake's elite social circle. "Flashes a perfect smile, and then she's gone," Melissa added.

"I swear," Larissa said, "some people live a charmed life."

Melissa eyed the beauty with contempt. "Right? Makes me want to wish a disfiguring disease on her to bring that goddess down to earth like the rest of us."

Christy Carmichael also worked her way through the crowd and nonchalantly came to a halt behind Larissa. Digging into her jeans pocket, she retrieved a small condiment package and let it drop to the floor. Melissa took notice of this and froze. "Ho bag, six o'clock," she said.

Larissa knew that could only mean one thing and started to glance over her shoulder. But before she could see what was about to transpire, she heard a foot stomp on the ground, then felt a wet splatter on her back. "Ketchup?" she asked Melissa with a cringe.

"Mustard," replied Melissa.

Larissa peered over her shoulder, as Christy folded her arms and waited for a response. Down by her feet lay the empty shell of an exploded mustard pack. Nearby students watched the two in anticipation. Larissa looked back at Melissa.

"Status?" she asked after a moment.

"Waiting," replied Melissa.

Larissa took a deep breath and grabbed her belongings.

"You know what? Today I'm not taking the bait." Without even glancing at her enemy, she stood and headed towards the nearest restroom.

Later that night, Larissa absently brushed her teeth. Her stomach felt like a bag of marbles. She didn't think she could take another night like the one before. After rinsing, she approached the toilet and peered inside. Just a regular run-of-the-mill toilet, or so it seemed.

Suddenly inspired, she grabbed a roll of toilet paper and unspooled the entire contents into the commode. Then, flushing the toilet, she watched it gurgle and clog.

Soon later, sliding into bed and pulling the covers up to her neck, Larissa crossed her fingers and prayed for an uneventful night's sleep.

Larissa opened her eyes many hours later to find the bedroom blanketed in early morning light. The clock read six twenty-five AM, and she inhaled deeply. There had been no dreams, no visitors. She got out of bed with an uncommon smile on her face.

While Larissa and Carter calmly ate their breakfast at the kitchen table, their father paced with the phone to his ear. "Can't you send someone out today? No, I don't know why." Gary set the phone on his shoulder.

"Kids, you didn't put anything down the toilet, did you?"

Carter shook his head.

"No tampons?" Gary asked.

Larissa shot him her best 'don't even go there' look.

"No, we don't know," he said into the phone.

Later, as the Westlake High student body arrived for class, Larissa sat on the steps drinking black coffee from a thermos. At her side, Melissa and Anthony were making out passionately. Larissa wondered if she and Lance ever looked so ridiculous with their public displays of affection. Across the courtyard, Christy flirted with some basketball jock. She noticed Larissa leering at her and shot her a cold sneer in return.

"It looks like Christy Carmichael's about to serve up another piping hot order of crabs," Larissa said.

Melissa pulled away from Anthony. "What?" she asked, clearly annoyed.

"Oh, never mind. As you were."

The couple resumed its interminable kiss. A few feet away on the steps, Larissa noticed a couple of nerdy teens huddled together while scrutinizing a tattered notebook. "So this is a visual representation of what the fourth dimension would look like," said the more pimply one of the clan, sketching with precision on the pad.

"What's it called again?" his friend asked.

"A tesseract."

Larissa looked over the nerd's shoulder at the drawing. It depicted a transparent cube within a cube.

"Just as there are infinite planes in a three dimensional world, there are infinite three dimensional spaces in the fourth dimensional world," the nerdy teen continued. The group then noticed Larissa eavesdropping.

"Far out," she offered.

The nerdy teen returned to his rapt colleagues. "Just as an entity from a two dimensional space isn't able to visualize a three dimensional world, we are incapable of visualizing a fourth dimension. Nevertheless, this drawing demonstrates conceptually how it works."

A few hours later, inside the guidance counselor's office opposite Ms. Patterson, Larissa doodled in her notebook. She sketched a cube within a cube.

"Tell me about your mom," Ms. Patterson said.

Larissa took a deep breath while the counselor patiently stood by for the reply. "Why?"

"Why not?"

"Because it's private."

"All the better."

"I don't see what she has to do with anything," she said in an attempt to bury the subject.

"My job is to assess if anything in your personal life is affecting your education," Ms. Patterson stated while leaning forward and placing her elbows on the desk. "I think she's important."

"You mean, you want to go laugh about her to your friends."

"That's not my idea of fun. Besides, unless violence

is involved, anything you say to me is strictly confidential according to our professional code of conduct."

Larissa looked at the clock.

"We've got 'til the end of the period," Ms. Patterson said.

All right, thought Larissa, she's got me. So, the student shifted in her seat in a failed attempt to get comfortable. "Over the summer my mom got really high-strung," she said. "You know, jumpy. She had a few panic attacks and she had a hard time..." Larissa suddenly became lost in thought.

"She had a hard time with what?"

"She had a hard time going to sleep. A doctor gave her some pills, but they didn't seem to work. She argued a lot with my dad, but I never could hear what it was about."

Ms. Patterson nodded and made a few scribbles in her notebook.

"Then one day, out of the blue, when we were at school, my mom tried to burn the house down. Some people came and took her away. Dad said she was going to be under observation for a while. That was two months ago."

Ms. Patterson closed her notebook.

"Happy now?" Larissa said, and then immediately regretted it.

"I'm sorry you and your family had to go through that. I can't imagine the stress involved."

Larissa nodded. She disliked the notion of others pitying her, regardless of the situation.

Ms. Patterson took off her glasses. "What happened to your mom can happen to just about anyone. I'm glad she's getting the help she needs. But, please don't give up on her. Right now I think your mother needs you to be her cheerleader. Don't throw in the towel. Okay?"

"Sure," the Larissa replied, praying for the bell to ring.

Six hours later, Larissa unspooled a roll of toilet paper into the toilet bowl and gave it a solid flush. Then, with the lights out, she sat at her computer and typed the words 'fourth dimension' into a search engine.

Based on the results, it appeared that two thoughts currently dominated the subject. One concept was that the fourth dimension existed not as a spatial dimension, but rather a temporal one, spacetime. The other described the fourth dimension as a purely spatial realm. Larissa clicked on a nineteen-seventies video narrated by cosmology guru Carl Sagan, which attempted to offer analogy as a means of imagining the fourth dimension. This video led her to another link on the tesseract.

"To form a tesseract," the narrator said. "We take the cube and drag it a distance L in the fourth dimension." She studied the mind-bending animation of a tesseract. "A four D world implies there are an infinite number of three D spaces adjacent to our own. In order to fully embrace this concept, we need to take a look at the logical progression of mathematics..." The tired teen rubbed her eyes, shut down the computer, and went to bed.

The idea of a powerful and intelligent species living in the sewer system underground, yet managing to remain undetectable all these years, seemed highly unlikely to Larissa. Perhaps these creatures did hail from another dimension. If so, how did they break through to our own? The world soon became fuzzy and Larissa drifted off to sleep.

When her eyelids parted, again she lay paralyzed in bed, engulfed in amber light. Scarface, Sunspots, Curly Locks, and Dark Eyes all encircled her. Unnerved as she was, Larissa made an attempt to keep her cool. "Where'd you come from?"

"You've been a naughty girl," said Scarface while shaking his head.

"Yeah, what's new?" she tossed back.

"There's more than one way in, Larissa," the leader added. "It's best you try not to cross us. We can make things uncomfortable for you. Very uncomfortable."

"I know what you look like. What you REALLY look like."

Scarface and Sunspots both smirked. Dark Eyes remained in the corner, silently eyeing her.

"You're nasty," Larissa said to them. "Butt ugly. Did anyone ever tell you that?"

"Are you trying to hurt our feelings?" Sunspots asked.

"And you reek," she added with venom.

"Sticks and stones may break my bones," said Curly Locks. Then he added with a chuckle, "If only we had these things you call bones."

Sunspots inserted a needle into her arm. Curly Locks held the fleshy bag, which began to fill with blood. "So what do you use it for?" she asked, motioning to the sac.

Scarface examined her pupils with the pink light. "Larissa, you are helping us a great deal. We are using your blood to develop a medicine. You see, where we come from, there is a terrible disease. There has been a tremendous amount of suffering, which you, thankfully, are helping to put an end to."

Dark Eyes spoke a few angry words and then approached to check her pulse. Larissa could tell Sunspots resented this gesture, perhaps because Sunspots was in theory the authority on all medical matters. "A disease, huh," the adolescent repeated aloud.

"I'm sure if your people were suffering, you would do anything you could to help them," Sunspots conjectured. "Wouldn't you?"

"Where do you come from?" Larissa asked. The four visitors exchanged a glance.

"It's very close," Curly Locks offered. "Closer than you would think. But it's very different."

"What do you mean?"

Dark Eyes released her arm. "We live in the sea," he said, apparently satisfied with her pulse.

Scarface barked a few words at Dark Eyes in their bizarre language. Sunspots then grabbed the fleshy tube and proceeded to insert it into her nostril. "When do you think you'll have enough blood?" she asked.

"There are many more sick to be treated," Scarface replied.

"But not to worry," Sunspots added. "Like we said, the procedure is perfectly safe."

With the tube in place, Larissa suddenly felt drowsy and her vision blurred. "Wait," she said. "Can we make a deal?"

"I don't think you're in any position to make a deal," laughed Curly Locks.

"If it's more blood that you need, maybe I can help."

"How is that?" asked Scarface.

"I can be pretty resourceful. Take this out of my nose, and I'll tell you."

Scarface motioned to Sunspots, who removed the tube from her nostril. The four figures looked to one another and debated.

"Do you want more blood or not?" she asked, teetering on the edge of unconsciousness.

"This is a very important matter, Larissa," said Scarface. "How do I know that we can trust you?"

"You'll leave me alone, and in return I'll find others for you. But you have to leave my brother and dad out of it. Clear?" Larissa took a deep breath and quickly felt more alert.

"What did you have in mind?" Scarface inquired, leaning in closer.

"Just listen..."

CHAPTER 7

The next morning, Larissa dragged her feet through the hallways of Westlake High, as tired and disheveled as she could ever remember. The students around her seemed to buzz with the energy that eluded her. She approached her locker, only to find the door swinging ajar.

"What the be-jesus?" she said to herself.

Melissa arrived and opened hers. "Que pasta?"

"Someone busted into my locker."

"Did they take anything?"

"I don't think so," Larissa answered taking a brief

survey of her belongings. "Good thing there's nothin' in here worth taking."

Melissa unearthed a tattered textbook from the bottom of her locker. "Yeah. Just stupid knowledge."

Later in fourth period, Larissa's fatigue made it difficult to concentrate on her sculpture. At her side, Brittany worked with fervor on the bulimic cheerleader. But when Brittany began whistling a tune, it was more than Larissa could bear.

"So, that slumber party you're having," Larissa began. "Is it just gonna be cheerleaders or what?

"You know, we're not as satanic as you might think," Brittany responded, not taking her eyes off her work. "Some of us actually have a sense of humor."

Larissa nodded, adding more paper mâché to her figure, which she determined would be a skateboarder.

"You interested?" Brittany asked after a moment of silence.

"Sure. Otherwise I'll be stuck at home with nothing to do."

"The lesser of two evils then, right?"

"Huh?" Larissa uttered, pretending not to know what she meant.

"Nothing. Glad you're coming."

That Saturday evening, with overnight bag in hand, Larissa rang the doorbell to Brittany's house, something she had not done in at least four years. "Sweet," Brittany chirped when she opened the door, moving aside to let her neighbor in. Larissa took a step inside just in time to see Mr. and Mrs. Welles pulling their coats from the closet.

"Hi, Larissa," Mrs. Welles said with an amiable smile.

"Hey, there," the awkward teen replied.

Mr. Welles looked to Brittany while putting on his charcoal overcoat. "Okay, honey, I've got my cell phone turned on." He then threw a look in Larissa's direction. "Hey, keep on eye on these girls for us. Make sure they don't run wild."

Larissa nodded with a smile. "I'll do my best."

Mr. and Mrs. Welles double checked they had everything they needed, then disappeared through the front door.

"Bring me back dessert!" Brittany screamed at them from the doorway.

"Night, ladies," Mr. Welles yelled back from the driveway.

Just then, a girl Larissa recognized appeared from the kitchen. Her name was Dana, a popular girl who had been in a few of Larissa's classes over the years. Larissa didn't recall Dana ever having spoken to her, and in fact, wasn't even sure Dana knew she existed.

"Hey, Larissa," Dana said. "I didn't know you and Brittany were neighbors."

Brittany and Larissa exchanged a glance. "Yep," was all Larissa could think to say.

"Larissa and I are in Biology together," Dana explained to Brittany. "Or, I should say Boreology."

As the evening elapsed, the six cheerleaders plus Larissa settled into the living room wearing sweat pants and pajamas. Two girls played a video game, while two others munched popcorn on the sofa. Larissa and Brittany sat cross-legged on the floor with Dana. The former petted Brittany's elderly basset hound, while Dana pulled two DVDs from her duffel bag. "While my dad wasn't looking, I swiped Toolbox Murders and Slumber Party Massacre."

Brittany took hold of Slumber Party Massacre. "This better be an improvement over the last one you brought over," she said flipping the case over and examining the artwork on back. "So PG-13."

A girl named Michelle entered with a plate of uncooked chicken breast and displayed them for Brittany. "The hens have marinated, master chef."

"Okay. Let's fire it up," Brittany announced.

Outside on the patio, Larissa watched as Brittany carefully placed the poultry on the barbecue grill. It was just the two girls standing together in the crisp evening air. Larissa's bra irritated her, so she reached back over her shoulder to scratch. Something caught Brittany's eye. "Is that what I think it is?" she asked.

"What?"

Brittany pointed with the tongs to her neighbor's shoulder. Larissa pulled her collar back slightly and realized that Brittany was looking at her Pisces tattoo.

"How on earth did you get away with that?" she begged to know.

"I was dumb enough to think my dad would never notice," Larissa said. "But he did. Grounded for a week."

"Wow. I wish I had the balls to do something like that."

"Yeah? Balls can sometimes weigh you down."

Brittany added some marinade to the chicken. "So I wanted to ask you something," she began cautiously. "My parents are going out of town next weekend, and I was thinking of having a little soirée. Do you think your dad'll call the cops if we get too loud?"

Larissa nodded without even having to think. "His middle name is buzz kill."

Brittany turned her lips upside down and pouted for a beat, at which point Larissa realized this must be her tactic for always getting everything she ever wanted. "Dear, dear," Brittany said flipping over some half-cooked birds.

"That is, unless someone accidentally drops a Benadryl into his Diet 7-Up," Larissa added.

Brittany studied her. "Why, we wouldn't want that to happen, would we?"

"Accidents happen," Larissa said shrugging.

The north end of the Welles home stood on an intersection, and the vacant house across the street was for sale. With the alley behind the house creating a modest sound barrier, it meant that Larissa's father may be the only person in the neighborhood potentially disturbed by raucous party noise.

Brittany turned the remaining chicken over and

laid the tongs aside. "What do you think the odds are of such an accident?"

"Well, I'll tell you this. I have real slippery fingers."

This last remark caused Brittany to snort.

Slumber Party Massacre progressed on-screen to the rapt attention of a few members of Westlake High's Cheerleading Squad. Larissa watched listlessly as the escaped mental patient chased voluptuous young women around with a prodigious power drill. Two of the other cheerleaders painted their nails, while another inflated an air mattress on the floor. Larissa watched the movie, then glanced at the clock; it was almost eleven.

After the movie, a tawdry gossip session erupted, the subject of which was the popular crowd at school. Naturally, Larissa didn't have much to add, but enjoyed listening to what life was like inside the inner circle. At one point, Brittany offered everyone some vodka from her dad's liquor cabinet, but only two girls took her up on it. They tried to drink one shot each, almost choked, and then spit up the clear liquid, giggling like twelve year-old girls. Mr. and Mrs. Welles eventually returned, and following a brief check-in, headed with their basset hound upstairs to turn in. Later, the girls fell asleep, scattered across the living room floor. That is, all except for Larissa. Amid the sound of soft snoring, she carefully crawled out of her sleeping bag, approached the nearest window, and cracked it open a few inches.

Sneaking out quietly through the front door and over to her house, Larissa grabbed one end of a garden hose and dragged it along the damp grass towards Brittany's yard. The creatures had pieced together a detailed map of the Locke residence plumbing network. All had agreed that instead of the upstairs toilet, the garden hose would serve as their exit this evening.

Once alongside the exterior of Brittany's living room, she took the end of the hose and threaded it through the window. Then, she quietly tiptoed back inside the house and to the living room where the girls slept peacefully. After checking to see the hose was securely hanging in the window frame, she headed for the kitchen.

Opening the Welles' fridge, Larissa snatched a Red Bull, and after taking a few sips, she sat down on the tile floor to wait. The digital clock on the wall read one seventeen AM. Everything was still—only the faint sound of crickets.

Larissa's mind traced back over the actions she had just taken and then leaped forward to the unsettling events about to transpire. To a large extent, she felt a sense of shame. Knowing that Brittany and her friends were about to be subjected to the same nightmare as herself gnawed at her conscience. In actuality, aside from perhaps ignoring her, none of these girls had really done anything wrong, at least not as far as Larissa was concerned. And even if they had, was that enough justification for what she had just done? Part of her still wondered why Brittany had even bothered to ask her over. Was it merely a ruse to prevent Larissa's dad from calling the cops during next week's rager? The notion irritated her. But possibly there was another reason. The friendliness that her neighbor had been projecting lately did seem genuine. Then again, perhaps Larissa was merely naive, and the cheerleader was in reality more manipulative than even Larissa had given her credit for. Hard to tell.

Larissa reassured herself that, although lethargic the next day, the girls would be fine. Then, she wondered to herself if it was possible for things to go awry. What if the paralysis was irreversible? What if they withdrew too much blood? What if someone was infected with a deadly virus? The idea made her stomach churn.

The rattle of a Coke can being knocked over made Larissa twitch. She looked at the clock again, two thirty-five. The creatures must be inside by now, she thought. They must have passed through as thin slippery eels and now were altering their anatomy in preparation to extract the blood. Larissa waited almost an hour in the same position until the clock read three twenty-seven, and at that moment she downed her second Red Bull.

At the sound of a creaking floorboard, Larissa looked through the kitchen door into the hallway. A shadow on the wall of one of the cricket-like creatures gracefully approached and then came to a stop. The figure compressed itself into a round blob, and then out from the shape emerged the resemblance of a human head. Soon, out from the sides emerged two lanky arms. The shadow then stood into the shape of a man. Larissa held her breath, and then into the kitchen walked Dark Eyes, a stoic expression on his face.

"You've done a good job. The others are happy."

"Are we done then?" she asked. "You have what you need?"

"You must be patient with us."

"Patient? Listen, if I'm gonna help you, I'm gonna need some answers," she said. "Are we done?"

"Please bear with us," he said. Dark Eyes then motioned to the living room. "I know the others can be quite... demanding."

Larissa was unsettled by the evasive nature of his response. "Tell me about this disease," she demanded.

A long awkward silence followed. Then from behind Dark Eyes, Curly Locks entered. The two figures acknowledged one another. "Good work, Larissa," Dark Eyes said in an authoritative tone. "Like I said, everyone is quite pleased."

"We'll see you again in two nights," Curly Locks added. "So be prepared."

"Two nights?" Larissa asked.

"Ta ta for now," he said. And without another word, the two beings retreated into the living room.

Later, just as the first rays of sun began to creep slowly through the trees, Larissa snuck outside to return the hose to its proper place. Then she reentered the living room to find everything just as she had left it. The girls were all asleep, scattered across the floor like discarded Barbies in a Malibu Dreamhouse. Paranoid, she leaned an ear close to each one to ensure they were still breathing. Satisfied, she approached her sleeping bag, crawled inside, and closed her eyes. Within two minutes, she was fast asleep.

CHAPTER 8

At ten AM, Mrs. Welles came into the living room to announce that she would be making pancakes for everyone. A few of the girls groaned in response. Larissa informed Mrs. Welles that she had to leave, and then bade farewell to Brittany, who waved from her sleeping bag while emitting a gaping yawn. After a speedy exit, Larissa opened the front door to her home and tiptoed to the stairs, trying not to arouse any attention. If I can just make it to my room, she thought.

"Hold on," her father yelled from somewhere in the house.

Larissa spun around to see Gary and Carter appear from the kitchen wearing jogging suits. "Sunday morning run," her father said with a humorless look on his face.

"I'm kinda tired," she replied, knowing perfectly well that putting up a fight with him always amounted to a waste of energy.

"Just because you stayed up late giggling with your girlfriends doesn't mean you get to skip your exercise. You've got five minutes."

Larissa stormed upstairs to change. After two hours of sleep, she now had to go running, her most loathed activity.

Twenty minutes later, Gary Locke led his children jogging through streets of the neighborhood, with Carter and his sister clearly short of breath. In fact, Larissa was breathing so heavily that her lungs ached. Having a rare shred of pity, their father came to a stop. Carter and Larissa bent over in agony. "Do you have any idea how embarrassing it is to be seen jogging with your dad and your little brother?" Larissa said.

"I'm not embarrassed," retorted her father.

"Why do you think I took up golf?" Carter interjected. "So I wouldn't have to break a sweat."

"Aerobic activity gets the blood pumping," Gary said. "Makes you feel good."

"Yeah," Larissa added. "I feel just great."

"Come on, let's keep going."

The kids didn't budge.

"Look alive," Gary said.

"Look normal," she replied.

"What?"

"Nothing."

Carter and Larissa reluctantly resumed the exercise and trailed their father down the street. They soon came upon their elderly neighbor, Mr. Sumi, who was riding his bicycle up the street in the opposite direction. Larissa slowed down to watch him pass, remembering what Curly Locks had said to her the night before about the creatures' upcoming visit.

Mr. and Mrs. Sumi had only lived in the neighborhood for a few years. Initially, they pretty much kept to themselves, never making an attempt to get to know the Locke children or their parents. After the incident with Larissa's mother, she noticed the Sumis become a lot more talkative with others in the neighborhood, taking every opportunity to visit with people whenever gardening outside. Eventually, they seemed to have a rapport with just about everyone... everyone, that is, except the Lockes.

A few weeks later, Larissa heard through the grapevine that the Sumis had spread gossip about them throughout the neighborhood. An incident that could've remained a private family matter soon became the talk of the community. Everyone was in the loop, and subsequently Larissa's family grew isolated.

Larissa looked over her shoulder at Mr. Sumi who teetered home on his rusty bicycle, and she knew right away that karma would be making a visit to his residence in a couple of days.

Monday morning came, and Larissa and Melissa walked to class through the drizzly parking lot. Melissa finished fixing her make-up in Larissa's pocket mirror and handed it back to her friend. "Joanna's gonna text me the answers to the Government quiz at nine," she said. "I'll pass 'em along."

"Awesome." Larissa noticed Lance's van with its signature "Lambert and Sons Nursery" insignia on the side pulling into an empty space ahead of them. "Ugh," she said. Lance exited the driver's side and offered her a friendly nod, but she ignored him and continued to school. "I spy with my little eye something that starts with the letter man-slut," she whispered to Melissa.

"According to Anthony, he's really not into Christy," Melissa replied. "Apparently it was a one-time thing."

"Is that supposed to make me feel better?"

"The guy made a mistake. Give him a break."

"What!? Are you suggesting we get back together?"

"I'm not suggesting that," Melissa said with more than a hint of frustration. "I'm just saying you can't let what happened ruin your entire year. At some point you're gonna have to let it go. For your own good."

Larissa couldn't help but roll her eyes. "Obviously, you've never been burned."

Melissa stopped. "You know, you're really good at playing the role of the 'angry girl.' But after a while, that gets old. Maybe it's time for an attitude adjust-

76

ment." The bell rang and Melissa continued to class without her.

Later in fourth period, Larissa worked on her sculpture next to an unusually lethargic Brittany Welles. The former was putting the finishing touches on her 'skateboarder,' when Mrs. Morales walked by. "I love the fact that you exaggerated the limbs," she said to Larissa. "You didn't try to create perfectly realistic form, but you gave it your own interpretation. Good work, Larissa."

"Thanks," she replied, surprisingly pleased with her own work.

Yawning, Brittany glanced at the clock. "Only eleven thirty! My God, will this day ever come to an end?"

Larissa couldn't think of a response. She could only hope that Brittany would snap out of her rut within a day or so.

During lunch that day, Larissa stared into space while Melissa rapid-fire texted on her phone. She couldn't tell if Melissa had some really important information to convey to someone, or if her BFF was merely avoiding having to talk with her. Then after lunch, Larissa found herself yet again seated across the desk from Ms. Patterson.

"Tell me about your father," the counselor began with a smile.

"He's a drill sergeant. Do this, do that. Don't do that. Typical."

"Why do you think he's like that?"

"Because he's a control freak."

"I felt the same way about my dad," Ms. Patterson said, taking off her sweater and stretching her arms in the air. "When I was your age I was notorious for dating the wrong guy. I was a sucker for the bad boy image. As a result, my father never let me out of his sight." Ms. Patterson took a look at the file folder on her desk. "You've had your share of behavioral issues. What does your father have to say about that?"

"He's embarrassed. Disappointed."

Ms. Patterson nodded. "Do you think he's worried about you?"

"I think he's worried about his image."

"Well, let's think about this. You're grown up. You're making choices on your own now. Soon you won't have him looking over your shoulder all the time. Do you think that the reason he's so controlling might be that he's worried about the choices you're going to make?"

Larissa looked out the window. "Don't know. Maybe."

"Because if that's the case, then perhaps his need to control you is his way of trying to protect you. After all, isn't that what fathers are supposed to do? Protect their children?"

"Well, maybe I'm not so interested in his protection. When do I get to make my own mistakes?"

"I understand, and I don't blame you. Just try to see things from his perspective, okay? That's all I'm asking."

The student nodded, and Ms. Patterson took a sip of coffee. In truth, Larissa wasn't used to putting herself into the shoes of others, least of all her father's.

In seventh period Biology class, Larissa kept on eye on Dana on the corner. Usually posture perfect and full of zest, today Dana rested her head on her arm, which extended lifeless across her desk. When moving her face to the side, a pale complexion and dark circles below the eyes revealed themselves to Larissa. In truth, although a little zonked out neither Dana nor Brittany seemed truly worse for wear, Larissa rationalized, reflecting on Saturday night's blood feast. Maybe it served Dana right, anyway. She had not spoken to Larissa at all that day. Not even a glimpse in her direction. Larissa surmised that Brittany's friends were the type to be chummy to your face, but once your back was turned, would throw shade in your direction. Maybe she's embarrassed to say hi, Larissa concluded.

When the last bell of the day rung, the class enthusiastically amassed its belongings. Funneling through the door, Larissa happened to come face to face with the groggy cheerleader. Snapping out of her daydream, Dana suddenly spotted Larissa. "Oh, hi. I like your shirt, Larissa," she said with a yawn. "Purple looks really good on you. You should wear that color more often."

"Well, thanks."

That night, the Locke family finished its lasagna dinner in silence. "Whose turn is it?" Gary asked.

Larissa stood and gathered the dirty dishes.

When her father's plate was removed, Gary noticed the laminated place mat underneath, which his daughter had fabricated at the age of six. Carter must have pulled it from the credenza when setting the table that evening. The place mat depicted an underwater scene with various fish and sea life. Gary held it up to admire its simple beauty, as Larissa collected the dirty silverware and pretended not to notice.

"I remember this. You made this in school, right?"

"Day camp," she replied.

"That's right." Gary returned the mat to the table. "That reminds me. A colleague of mine at work was saying that the arts college on the other side of the bay has a solid reputation. You might want to think about applying next year. I'm sure you could put together a stellar portfolio."

"Yeah? I'll think about it," she said; and she genuinely meant it.

"Good."

Larissa rinsed the dishes in the sink and started the dishwasher. The idea of going to art school certainly aroused her interest. Unsure whether she would be able to maintain a career as an artist someday, she could at least pursue her passion in art school without having the dreadful academics crammed down her throat.

After cleaning up the kitchen, Larissa dragged the trash bin and recycle container to the street corner. Looking up, she observed the sun setting behind the roofs of the neighboring houses. A particularly frosty breeze picked up and made her shiver.

She noticed her neighbor Mr. Sumi dragging his bins to the street. The two shared an awkward moment of silence. "Nice night," he said.

"Nice night for what?" Larissa asked.

Mr. Sumi thought for a moment and was about to reply, but before he could, she turned her back and returned inside.

At around ten-thirty that night, Larissa finished flossing her teeth and peered out the bathroom window. Next door, Mr. and Mrs. Sumi could be seen washing dishes in their kitchen window. They soon completed their task and turned out the lights. As the Sumis disappeared from view, all the windows in their house proceeded to go black.

Larissa tiptoed down the hallway and past her father's dark and quiet room. She crept down the stairs and slipped silently out the back door. Outside, she took the hose and dragged it across the lawn, just like she had done the Saturday before. However this time, she headed south to the Sumi residence.

Approaching their back door, she searched behind a planter and retrieved what looked like a grey stone. Turning the stone over in her hand revealed the plastic door she was looking for. On a few occasions in the past, Larissa happened to observe the Sumi's house sitter when the couple vacationed out of town. She remembered the location of their spare key in the event she might need it, and tonight was unquestionably the night. She slid the plastic compartment open to claim possession of the key.

After surveying the somber household, Larissa unlocked the back door. Entering her neighbor's home provided a sudden rush of adrenaline. As a car drove by outside, the headlights shined though the windows, briefly illuminating her unfamiliar surroundings. Asian paintings hung on the walls. A collection of geisha dolls posed on display in glass containers on the book shelf. The teen was briefly startled by a ghoulish traditional Asian mask hanging on the wall.

Larissa continued toward the front of the house. Seemingly out of nowhere, Mr. Sumi rounded the corner and nearly bumped into his intruder. Luckily, his eyes had not yet adjusted to the dimness. Looking downward, he walked right past Larissa and disappeared into the kitchen. The girl froze, her heart pounding against the inside of her rib cage.

She watched him fetch a glass of water from the sink, but when she took a step backwards into the living room, the floorboards creaked. Mr. Sumi uttered something sharply in Japanese.

Larissa ducked behind a leather armchair. Mr. Sumi entered the room gripping a cleaver in his right hand and switched on the light. From upstairs, Mrs. Sumi yelled something to her husband, and he hollered back in return. Mr. Sumi surveyed the living room and approached the arm chair where Larissa hid. To remain out of sight, she crawled around to the other side of the chair, realizing that only one unlucky creak of a floorboard would betray her presence. She wasn't sure what she would say if Mr. Sumi discovered her; she just prayed he wouldn't whack her in the head with his cleaver.

Then, Mr. Sumi took one last look around, turned out the lights, and retreated upstairs. Larissa paused for a moment to catch her breath. She resolved that breaking and entering was decidedly not her thing. After a few minutes, she tiptoed to the kitchen and cracked open the window. Then returning outside, she fed the hose in through the kitchen window and waited. Within just a few seconds, the hose twitched, and she saw the shape of a long tentacle slithering through.

Larissa stood there for a while as the four creatures passed in through the window. Then she took a seat on a tree stump in the back yard and gazed up at the stars. She wondered if her adult life would continue to prove as challenging as the teenage years. Her father had once told her that high school years are often the best of a person's life. Ha! She attempted to tap into any ESP that she may possess in order to elicit a glimpse of the future, but unfortunately no clear vision presented itself. About an hour later, the tentacles slid back up the hose, and she knew the deed had been done.

When she returned home through the kitchen, she stumbled upon Carter standing in front of the open fridge searching for a midnight snack. He frowned at Larissa and shook his head. "I don't suppose you were out late selling Girl Scout cookies," he said.

His sister shrugged. "Sorry. Not everyone can be perfect."

"Can't you just not be a train wreck for, like, five

minutes? Do you know how dull it is listening to Dad constantly complain about your poor decision-making skills?"

"Oh, you poor thing. Maybe you should mind your own pre-pubescent business." She realized the she was on the brink of yelling, so she lowered her voice. "You have no clue. You really don't."

When Larissa eventually pulled the covers up to her chin, she asked herself what she might do if the creatures demanded more blood. Although she prayed the Sumis were the last, she acknowledged a sinking suspicion that her visitors would continue to ask for more. Having already taken advantage of her neighbors on both sides, a third series of victims would prove more complicated. How would she transport the creatures to another location? Would she be reduced to luring victims into her own home?

The next morning, the buzz of her alarm clock roused Larissa from a deep sleep. She pulled herself out of bed and rubbed her crusty eye sockets. Approaching the window, Larissa noticed an ambulance parked outside on the street in front of the Sumi house. Snatching a coat, she resolved to get a closer look.

Hugging the corner of the house by her front door, Larissa had a clear vantage point of the Sumi residence. After a few minutes, two paramedics wheeled Mrs. Sumi out of the house in a stretcher and down the driveway to the back of the ambulance. A weary-eyed Mr. Sumi followed and then held his wife's hand for a moment on the street. He spoke to her, but Larissa could not detect whether his wife's eyes were open or closed, or if she spoke back. The paramedics interrupted Mr. Sumi and lifted his wife into the rear of the vehicle. Larissa became aware that she was biting her nails as the ambulances doors closed. Mr. Sumi took a seat in the front of the ambulance, and the vehicle took off, sirens blaring, through the early morning mist.

Larissa understood at that moment that she had helped the creatures for the very last time. Logically, she felt she should have no sympathy for the Sumis, and yet the sick feeling in the pit of her stomach indicated otherwise. Perhaps she felt disappointment in herself for having acted like the girl everyone expected her to be, a self-absorbed troublemaker with no empathy or consideration for others. It seemed high time to redirect the energy she had applied toward assisting her nocturnal visitors and aim it toward planning their demise.

CHAPTER 9

Larissa entered Westlake High on Thursday morning along with the horde of other unenthusiastic students. A crowd amassed at a wall near the main office where the janitor was painting over some graffiti. The students all laughed uncontrollably at the illustration of Mr. Miller with his mouth open, a large penis directed inside.

On the way to her locker, Larissa passed in front of the art room, where the completed sculptures stood on display. She noticed Lance lingering to admire her skateboarder. He spun around and spotted his ex. "Not bad," he said after a beat. "Why a skateboarder?"

"It's my alter-ego."

"Really?" he said. "I didn't know that."

"Well," she said avoiding eye contact, "unfortunately wheels and I don't exactly get along. I have no sense of balance. You know, total disaster."

Lance nodded, and subsequently the tardy bell put an end to their strained conversation. "Well, I'll see ya later," he said.

"See ya," she replied.

Later in the lunch line, Larissa and Melissa amassed food on their plastic trays. "And if Anthony gets into the Tech Institute," Melissa said, "he'll only be forty-five minutes away. Not bad, huh?"

"They're out of chocolate milk," Larissa noticed. She grabbed an order of fries and observed Brittany Welles strut nearby to pluck an apple from the fruit bowl.

"Hey, Larissa," she said. The cheerleader appeared rosier than the last time Larissa had seen her.

"What's up?" Larissa offered in return, relieved at her neighbor's renewed vivacity.

"Oh, the u-zhe."

Melissa rolled her eyes as Brittany bounced over to the cashier. "What, are you Ms. Perfect's bitch now?" she inquired.

"She's actually not that bad, you know."

"Please. The only reason she's nice to you is because she's jealous of your bad girl image."

"I swear," Larissa said, trying not to lose her patience, "sometimes the lamest things come out of your mouth. Can't you give anyone credit for just being a nice person?"

"Spare me. When was the last time you won a Nobel Peace Prize?" Melissa headed to the register, leaving her friend to munch on a soggy fry.

Near the end of the day, while the rest of seventh period biology class watched a video on marine mammals, Larissa lost herself in a daydream. Her left hand absently doodled on the note pad in front of her. Mrs. Sumi dominated her thoughts, and Larissa hoped that her neighbor's health would soon return to normal. After what the Sumis had done to her family, Larissa was surprised at how guild-ridden she felt. Despite a need to exact revenge on her gossipy neighbors, in the end vengeance did not feel as cathartic as she had predicted. Perhaps Mrs. Sumi suffered from a health condition that made the extraction of blood dangerous, if not fatal. The thought had not previously occurred to her, otherwise she would have followed an alternate course of action.

"Like several of its amphibian cousins, the salamander is equipped with both gills and lungs," the narrator of the video proclaimed, "making it possible to hunt for food both on land and in water." This caught Larissa's attention, so she directed her focus to the TV screen. "Whereas marine mammals do not have gills and must return to the surface periodically for oxygen. The Northern Bottlenose whale can hunt for as long as thirty minutes under water before coming up for air."

She pondered this for a beat and resumed her sketch, a drawing of one of the creatures inside a tesseract. She remembered Dark Eyes commenting that they hailed from the sea, but they spent at least an hour at night outside the water. Could they remain outside the water indefinitely, or did they need to return to the sea just like dolphins need to return to the surface for air? If they indeed needed to return within a fixed period of time, how long could they stay on dry land?

An aide entered and handed a slip of paper to the science teacher. "Larissa, it's for you," Mr. Dressler said. She took the slip and read it over, a request to visit the assistant principal. Oh, joy, she thought. What could it be this time?

When Larissa arrived at Mr. Miller's office with the slip in hand, the assistant principal was in the middle of a phone conversation. He motioned for her to sit, so she plopped down in the same seat she had found herself in a few weeks earlier.

"I have to run," he barked into the phone. "There's a student here. Take care." Mr. Miller hung up, folded his hands, and looked the teen in the eye. "Larissa, do you know why I asked you here today?"

She shook her head.

"Did you happen to see what was painted on the wall this morning?" he asked.

Larissa tried not to smile. "I did."

Mr. Miller stared her down, and there was an uneasy moment of silence.

"Wait a second," Larissa said. "You don't think that was me, do you?" She suddenly felt a lump in her throat. "Seriously, I have no beef with you. I know you were just doing your job."

Mr. Miller nodded. "The custodian found something this morning that was left near the graffiti. Are you missing anything?"

"Nope." Her mind was racing. Was she missing something?

Mr. Miller reached into his desk and retrieved her hoodie. "Does this belong to you?"

"Yeah," she said in a state of shock. "I didn't know it was even gone."

Mr. Miller returned it to his drawer.

"You know what?" Larissa said, trying not to stammer. "My locker was broken into last week. The lock's completely busted. Whoever took it must've... You can go take a look at my locker right now."

"I don't think that will be necessary," Mr. Miller said folding his hands again on the desk and regarding her with a touch of pity. She stared back at him, perplexed.

"You don't believe me do you? You can go take a look."

"We have an eye witness."

"What? That's bullshit. Who? Is it Christy Carmichael or one of her cronies?"

Mr. Miller didn't respond, but looked away. Then, he leaned back in his squeaky chair and inhaled deeply. "Under the circumstances, I'm afraid..."

"No! Wait, you can't be serious."

"I'm afraid I have no choice..."

"I've been set up! It's so obvious!"

"But to expel you."

Larissa froze.

"I spoke to your father a short while ago. He's on his way here."

After of hour-long yelling match between Larissa and her father, she ran to her bedroom and slammed the door. Larissa collapsed onto the bed, burying her face in the pillow. Gary burst through. "Don't walk out while I'm talking to you," he shouted.

"What is there left to say?"

Her father flung a pamphlet on the bed. "Take a look at your new home." She lifted her head to glance at it, a boarding school brochure. "Congratulations. You'll be miles away from your dear old dad. I guess you got what you always wanted." Gary stormed out and left his daughter alone to sulk. She tried to control the tears, but they wouldn't hold back. Wiping them away, she noticed Carter standing in the doorway.

"Did you do it?" he asked.

"People will believe what they want."

"I'm asking if you did it."

She looked Carter in the eye. "No."

"That sucks."

Larissa nodded.

"Now you're going to leave me all alone here with Dad? Are you kidding me?" He turned in a huff and headed to his room, leaving Larissa staring at the empty door frame.

Larissa sat in bed for the next hour looking up at the ceiling. Her best guess was that she would be leaving for boarding school within a few days, so she didn't have much time to act. And if she didn't act, Carter would be left to the whims of the malicious creatures.

At that moment Larissa started to concoct her plan. It began merely as the germ of a plan, but at least she had something. More than anything, it was an acknowledgment that something needed to happen quickly. Immediately she came to realize that she needed help. Specifically, she needed someone with a car. Larissa toyed with the idea of talking to Melissa, but immediately reconsidered. Melissa was her best friend, but if she thought Larissa had lost her marbles, their friendship could be forever jeopardized. It's amazing that one could spend nine years building a bond with someone, only to destroy it with a few far-fetched words. On the other hand, Larissa thought, if Melissa really cared about their friendship, she would give her the benefit of the doubt. She would at least allow Larissa the opportunity to prove her sanity.

She picked up her cell phone and dialed. After two rings, Melissa answered. "Hey, you."

"Hi. You got a sec? I could use your help."

"I'm on the phone with Anthony. Can I call you later?"

"You know, I don't even know why I bother anymore."

"What's with you?"

"I hope you and Anthony have a nice life."

"Larissa..."

Larissa threw the phone onto her bed. She chickened out. It was pointless. Melissa clearly had other priorities. She got dressed for bed, turned out the light, and sat in the darkness for quite some time.

When she opened her eyes, she instantly became aware of Dark Eyes standing before her alone. Larissa bolted upright. "Dude, you're creepy."

"I can't stay long," he said. "When the others find out that I came through by myself, they'll be angry."

"What the eff?" she said. "You said nobody would get hurt."

"I know. That was unfortunate. So, I came to warn you."

"Warn me?"

"The others, they are out of control."

"What do you mean?"

There was a brief pause, then Dark Eyes came closer. "At first it started innocently, but now they're insatiable. Their judgment is... off."

"Insatiable? I don't get it? I thought this was about a disease. How much more do you need?" Dark Eyes was about to speak, but then hesitated. Larissa noticed his gaze drift downward, seeming to avoid contact with her own. "There is no disease, is there?" she asked.

"There is no disease. Your blood is like a drug. It drives our kind wild. The others, they can't seem to get enough. I've put up with it for a while, but now they won't stop."

"Why are you telling me this?"

"Like your kind, not one of us is the same. Some are naturally gifted in science or language. I have the ability to experience what others feel, simply be being in their presence. I can feel their joy, sadness, and terror."

Larissa nodded, sitting up in bed. Dark Eyes' empathetic nature apparently stood out as a unique trait among his ilk. And although she appreciated the lowdown, the greater understanding of her predicament did little to diminish its burden.

"What's happening won't end unless you put a stop to it," Dark Eyes added.

"I want to, but I don't know how."

"You have to find a way. If you don't, what lies ahead could be disastrous." The visitor turned to leave.

"Hey," Larissa said. "Tell me what it's like. Where you're from."

Dark Eyes stopped in the doorway. "Would you like to see it?"

Larissa nodded. "Yeah."

"Then close your eyes."

She obeyed. Dark Eyes approached the bed and placed his hand on her forehead.

Although Larissa understood she remained in bed with her eyes closed, it was suddenly as if she was somewhere else. A vision came to her, and she found herself propelled through a labyrinth of underwater tunnels. "We created an entryway into your world," Larissa heard Dark Eyes say. "Our first few attempts led us to arid land. But the last time we broke through to water, which gave us an opportunity to explore."

Larissa's vision became blinded by an immense flickering blue light. The next thing she knew, she was hovering in front of a vast panorama of the sea. However, this was unlike any other sea she had seen before; this one glowed a bright aqua blue. She hovered above it, gliding in the breeze. A myriad of rugged islands jutted above the surface of the water at her sides. From their silvery rock rose asymmetrical bushes composed of twisted purple branches and yellow thorns, reaching longingly to the heavens. She gasped at the beauty of it all.

"What do you think?" Larissa heard Dark Eyes say.

"I can't believe what I'm seeing."

She then dove under the surface of the sea. Strange creatures whisked by, translucent and eel-like in nature, but so fast that she couldn't get a clear look. Approaching the bottom of the sea, she saw an endless village of rock, like that of the Incan Empire she had seen photos of in last year's World History class. Creatures scurried in and out of doors and windows. They carried things, they built things, they talked, they fought. In many ways, it was a city like any other.

"You did a fantastic job the other night, Larissa."

The teenager opened her eyes. Sunspots stood before her with a needle in his hand. Scarface and Curly Locks approached her side. Dark Eyes was nowhere to be seen.

"Haven't you had enough?" she said, feeling the paralysis set in, her vision growing bleary.

"I'm afraid this is only the beginning," Scarface replied. "There are many more sick to be treated."

Sunspots thrust the needle in her arm. She winced. "Yeah, I'm sure."

"We were wondering when we might be able to take advantage of your services again," Scarface added.

"It's not that easy," she replied. "I need some time."

"You're a resourceful girl," he said. "You'll put something together. We'll be back at eleven tomorrow night. I'm sure you won't disappoint us."

As the fleshy bag filled with her blood, a reluctant tear slid from her eye.

CHAPTER 10

Larissa's eyes squinted apart to the daylight streaming in through the window. She coerced herself out of bed and to the vanity mirror. God, she looked like a hot mess. At the sound of an engine turning over, she peeked out the window and saw her father's car back out of the driveway and head for work. Good riddance, she thought.

Down in the kitchen, Larissa seized the chore list off of the fridge, crumpled it up, and tossed it in the garbage. Then, she proceeded to make herself a strong cup of black coffee. She sat at the kitchen table drinking joe and thinking about her plan to thwart the night visitors, which was coming together piece by piece. She sought to isolate them away from the house, preferably somewhere away from the water. She didn't know how long they could survive outside the water before having to return, but it seemed like a good way to make them more vulnerable. She also needed a car; that was the tricky part.

Larissa took the bus that morning to the Winchester Hospital. She wished to say goodbye to her mother, not knowing when she would see her next, but she also had a question that was turning over in her mind. It seemed odd that her mother should be the one incarcerated in a mental hospital, when ever since Larissa could remember, her mother grounded the family in emotional stability. Roberta Locke had a knack for softening Gary during his temper tantrums, and she certainly didn't fuel the fire while Larissa was passing through the roller coaster middle school years. Whenever emotions would run wild in the Locke household, Roberta Locke would simply bake a banana bread and all would sort itself out.

After a good hour, the bus pulled up alongside the cream-colored edifice, the doors swung open, and Larissa stepped out onto the sunny sidewalk. Passing through the sliding glass doors, she headed to the reception. "Hi, I'm Larissa Locke," she said to a tiny brunette. "I'm here to see Roberta Locke."

The receptionist reviewed the clipboard in front of her. "Did you call ahead of time?"

"No, I wasn't able to. Is it possible to see her?"

"Visiting hours are almost over," she said with a

sigh. "But go ahead and sign in."

After the receptionist buzzed her in, Larissa passed through the double doors and down the sterile hallway leading to the visiting area. This large, rectangular room consisted of three rows of plain wooden tables. Patients and visitors sat opposite one another, conversing. A male nurse went to fetch Roberta, while Larissa took a seat at the end of one of the tables. A voice came through the loudspeaker, "Visiting hours will come to a close in ten minutes."

Wow, that's not much time, Larissa thought. She then wanted to kick herself in the pants for not planning her time better.

The nurse soon ushered a disheveled Roberta Locke inside. Larissa immediately felt a surge of emotion at seeing her mother in such an unpolished state. Recognizing her daughter, Roberta offered a nervous smile and gave Larissa a hug. Larissa could tell solely from this brief encounter that her mother had changed quite a bit over the past few months. First the apprehensive smile, and then upon hugging her, Larissa could tell that her strength had waned. The two sat down and held hands across the long wooden table. Roberta wore a traditional hospital gown. Her eyes moved constantly from Larissa, to the window, and back down to her hands. "How's Carter?" she asked feebly.

"Carter is the same as always," Larissa responded. "I'm sure he'll cure cancer by the time he's fifteen. And Dad, well, he's been cranky. Which is another way of saying he's the same as always, too."

Roberta asked how everyone was eating and wanted to make sure someone was watering the azaleas. Several minutes passed in awkward conversation between the two. Larissa informed her mother about boarding school, but this news seemed to make little impact on Roberta. After a minute of silence Roberta offered a brief smirk and then returned to looking out the window. "I'm sorry, honey. They keep me so medicated. Because of everything they pump into me, I... sometimes it's hard to focus. What I wouldn't give for a good night's sleep. You can't believe how hard it is to sleep in a place like this."

"I haven't been sleeping so good, either," Larissa said.

There was an uneasy pause. "I am happy you came," Roberta said at last.

"Mom, when you were at home, did you ever see anything strange?"

For the first time, Larissa's mother looked her squarely in the eye. "Strange?"

"I mean, did you ever see something that wasn't supposed to be there? And wondered if it was real?"

She regarded Larissa cautiously. "What do you mean? You haven't been sleeping well, have you?"

"No. Like I said, I haven't."

Roberta was on the verge of divulging something, but a nurse passed by. Larissa leaned forward, whispering.

"Did you ever see any... visitors?"

Roberta hesitated and scanned the room suspiciously before returning her gaze to Larissa. "You saw them?"

"I have, Mom. I have. I don't think you're crazy."

A tear slid down Roberta's cheek. She grabbed tightly onto Larissa's arm and sobbed. "I'm so confused. I don't know what's real anymore. They tell me they aren't. They tell me..." Roberta bit her lip.

"They're real, Mom. I know now just as well as you."

Larissa rolled up her sleeve and discreetly revealed to her mother a scar on her arm.

Roberta gasped. "What did they do to you?"

"Don't worry. I'm gonna fix it, or at least try."

"I'm so sorry, honey. I'm sorry I left you in this mess. I tried to do something."

"Is that why you tried to torch the house?"

Roberta nodded, unable to prevent the tears from flowing. "Honey, you have to be careful. They're very dangerous."

The voice returned to the loudspeaker. "Visiting hours are now over. Please exit the visiting room."

Patients and guests rose. Roberta and her daughter hesitated, then reluctantly stood. They made their way around the table and embraced. "I love you," Roberta said. "But now I'm so worried."

"I love you too, Mom. Try not to worry." Two double doors opened and three hospital attendants entered the visiting area to escort patients back into the ward. "And I'm going to help get you out of here," Larissa asserted.

"You think so?"

"Just don't say anything more about this."

Roberta grabbed Larissa's hand and kissed it. She leaned in and whispered in her daughter's ear. "I had a drink one night. I remember it made them ill. Really ill."

"What do you mean?"

"A white Russian. I think it was a white Russian. My memory isn't what it used to be."

An attendant approached. "It's time to say good-bye, Mrs. Locke."

Roberta nodded, then turned to Larissa. "Use it to your advantage."

"How?"

"You'll think of something." Roberta gave her a quick kiss on the cheek. Larissa waved as the attendant escorted her mom through the double doors and out of sight.

Moments later, Larissa stood in a daze at the bus stop until the bus rolled up and opened its doors. She felt a surge of relief that her mother was not mentally ill. And if her mother was not out of her mind, then perhaps in a matter of time, Roberta could convince the doctors to release her. A White Russian, though? How does that fit into the equation?

Soon later, when the bus passed by the Lambert and Sons Nursery, an idea suddenly popped into Larissa's head. She yanked the chord, indicating the driver to stop. The adolescent jumped out onto the sidewalk and jogged to the nursery, where she spotted Lance's older brother, Randall, watering some plants.

"Haven't seen you in a while," he said upon noticing her.

"I know. Is your brother working this afternoon?"

"He's out on a delivery."

Larissa pulled a note from her pocket and handed it to her ex's sibling. "Could you give this to Lance for me?"

"Sure."

"'Preciate it."

An hour later, Larissa walked past the Sumi house on her way home. Although not wanting to appear too conspicuous, she slowed her pace in an attempt to discern if anyone was home. Three days had passed without any sign of the couple. Unfortunately, the windows were dark and beheld no signs of life.

Later, she rummaged through the cluttered garage while trying to position a cell phone to her ear. "Hello?" the school secretary said from the other end of the line.

"Hi, I'm calling for Ms. Patterson."

"Who may I ask is calling?"

After a moment's hesitation, "Larissa Locke."

"One second."

Larissa found a box of matches in a utility drawer and set it aside.

"Hello, Larissa," Ms. Patterson said.

"Hi."

"Look, since you're no longer a student here, I'm afraid I'm not going to able to advise you."

"I didn't do what they said I did. And I just wanted to ask you one more question, since you seem to have a lot of answers."

Ms. Patterson hesitated.

"What are you supposed to do when the world shuts you out?" Larissa asked.

"That's tough. I guess it depends. Sometimes being on the outside isn't always a bad place to be."

"What do you mean?"

"You get a unique perspective on things. You're able to make observations that those on the inside cannot. And in the end, you'll likely become more self-reliant."

"Small consolation."

"Perhaps. Maybe some day down the road you'll have a greater understanding of what you're going through right now. A mentor of mine once said that it's possible to veer so far off the beaten path that the world around you will close its doors on you. But only at that point will you truly know that you're walking in the path God has intended."

Larissa nodded to herself, not quite convinced.

"And I'm afraid that's going to have to be enough."

"I see."

"Good luck. And Larissa..."

"Yeah."

"I do believe you. And I believe in you."

While Ms. Patterson could do nothing to alter the current situation, Larissa found a ray of hope in the notion that at least one member of the human race still had faith in her. "Thanks. Bye."

Larissa hung up and then stumbled upon what she was searching for, a dusty gas can hiding on the back of a shelf behind some turpentine. Lugging it from its spot, she could tell by the weight that the can was almost full. She laid it on the floor next to the matches. When exiting the garage, she saw two jocks carrying a keg into Brittany's house next door. Party time was drawing near.

Larissa logged onto her Facetime account. On the computer screen, Brittany appeared looking all dolled up and ready for a good time. Once she caught sight of Larissa, she put on that pout of hers. "Hey, Larissa," she said.

"I'm afraid I can't come over tonight."

"I'm sure. I heard about what happened. That's unbelievable."

"Tell me about it."

"Is there anything I can do?"

"Just have a good time."

Larissa held up a Diet 7 Up can and a package of Benadryl, and then dumped two pink pills into the fizzing soda can. "Whoops."

Brittany laughed. "I owe you one, you crazy bitch. You are by far the best neighbor I have ever had."

The waxing moon blanketed Walnut Creek in a silvery shimmer. Next door, a handful of teenagers strolled up the driveway to Brittany's house, where the music thumped to an electric beat.

Larissa left her bedroom and tiptoed across the hall. She cracked open the door to Carter's room and peeked inside.

Decked out in a pair of headphones, Carter teed off on his favorite Tiger Woods video game. Closing the door, she continued down the hallway and entered her father's room. Fully dressed, Gary dozed on his bed next to an open book and the laced soda can. She glanced at the clock on the wall, ten seventeen PM. She had less than an hour. Silently, she slipped out.

A few minutes later, and only five blocks away, the sound of knocking on glass drew Lance to his bedroom window. Upon pulling open the blinds, he found Larissa on the other side of the glass. He offered a warm smile and slid the window open to let her inside.

"The refugee in the flesh," he said.

"Wow. Déja vu."

"Mi casa es su casa."

Lance thanked her for the note and asked if she wanted a hit off his water bong, which she refused. "You know it makes me mega paranoid," Larissa reminded him.

"I'm just not ready to do the whole boyfriend girlfriend thing," Lance said while packing a bowl. "I'm too young to get all serious and stuff. We have our whole lives for that."

"But seriously," she replied, "of all people, Christy Carmichael?" Larissa laughed.

"I know, I know. I don't know what I was thinking. I wasn't thinking." Lance took a hit off the bong.

"Well, I'm glad we can still be friends," she assured him.

Lance nodded and patted her on the knee just like he used to do. "I'm so glad you're not mad at me anymore. Mad sucks."

Larissa leaned forward to give him a kiss, and the two made out for a few seconds.

"Hey, does your dad have any beer?" she asked.

"I... I don't know. You want me to go check?"

"Yeah."

Lance gave her one more kiss and exited the room. Larissa noticed the clock, ten fifty-seven. She quickly stood and snatched Lance's keys off the hook on the wall. She was counting on them being there, and they didn't disappoint. She jotted the word "sorry" on his dry erase board and slid through the window open. Dropping to the ground with the keys in hand, she hurried to the large white van with "Lambert and Sons Nursery" stenciled on the sides. She started the vehicle and peeled out of the driveway.

Moments later, Larissa pulled the white van to a stop in the dark alley behind her house. So far, events had progressed just as planned, albeit a little late. She stormed into her room to discover fifteen men including Scarface, Sunspots, and Curly Locks all milling about. Oddly, they all resembled popular professional golfers and appeared highly agitated.

"It's about time," Scarface said.

"It's like the whole freakin' PGA in here. Come on."

After quietly leading them down the stairs and out the back, Larissa pulled the back door to the van open, revealing a small windowless space filled with a few scattered plants.

Scarface and the other men wore a dubious expression.

"Let's go," she said nonchalantly.

Scarface and Sunspots swapped a few words in their foreign tongue. Then, Scarface turned to the teen. "You never mentioned this."

"Where we're going is too far to walk. It's only a five minute drive. Plus, we can't be seen. Trust me. This is the only way."

Scarface paused and looked to the others. Curly Locks said something and a few of the men laughed. Scarface grinned. "All right. Let's go." The men piled into the back and Larissa pulled the door closed, latching it shut. She hopped in the driver's seat and peeled away, but immediately came to a grinding halt.

A pick-up truck belonging to Lance's brother Randall pulled into the alley blocking the exit. Lance stepped out of the passenger seat. "You're in deep shit," he said.

Larissa switched the car into reverse and hit the accelerator. Lance hopped back in the pick-up, shaking his head in disbelief. Performing a speedy three-point turn, she exited the alley and burst out onto the suburban street. Her desired destination was south – the vast empty parking lot of a shuttered department store. She maneuvered the van adeptly through the sleepy neighborhood.

A red light forced Larissa to brake. The pick-up pulled up in the lane next to her, windows rolled down. "Pull over now!" Lance yelled.

"I'm calling the cops," Randall added, holding a cell phone to his ear. She noticed a minivan pull up behind the pick-up. "Dude, you're gonna be so sorry," Lance goaded.

Larissa shifted into reverse and sent the van lurching backwards. Then pulling off a smooth one-eighty, she took off in the opposite direction. The pick-up scrambled to follow.

A few blocks away, she pulled the van into an empty park. A knocking sound became audible behind her head. "It's okay," Larissa yelled back. "Don't worry. We had to take a little detour." She came to an abrupt stop at the end of the parking lot near a small pond. This obviously wasn't her planned location, but given the circumstances, it would have to do. She got out and darted to the passenger side, where she retrieved the dusty gas can. She sloppily splashed gasoline onto the vehicle, and then pulled the box of matches from her pocket. Shaking, she attempted to light the matches, but the wind proved too brisk.

Suddenly, the pick-up pulled into the parking lot and jerked to a stop. A match ignited in Larissa's hand and she took a step toward the van. Lance flew out of the truck and toward his ex-girlfriend, and then the match flickered out. Lance knocked the matches out of her hand. "What has gotten into you?!" he screamed. She bent over to pick them up, but Lance snatched them out of her hand. "Stop!" he yelled. "You have lost your mind!" Larissa struggled to get the matches from Lance, but she tripped over a root and fell backwards onto the damp grass. "I don't know what I was thinking hanging around a pathetic psycho like you," Lance blurted while heading back toward the van.

"Wait..." Larissa said, trying to pull herself up.

Randall leaned out the pick-up window. "Don't you ever come anywhere near my family again," he said. He then peeled out and the pick-up disappeared in a cloud of exhaust.

Larissa began to cry out of panic and frustration. "Wait..."

Lance entered the van and turned the ignition. Once the vehicle started, he turned the van around and rolled down the window. "You've lost it, man. Like mother, like daughter. How does it feel to lose your mind? Freakin' lunatic."

"Stop!" Larissa yelled finally rising to her feet, when she heard a loud crashing sound emanate from inside the van. A cricket-like appendage punctured a hole into the cabin from the back and wrapped around Lance's neck. She froze in her tracks, watching Lance gasping desperately for air. In one fell swoop, the appendage pulled him back through the hole and out of sight. A muffled shriek erupted from the back of the van, and then all fell silent.

Larissa bolted toward the park's exit. Glancing behind her, she saw several cricket-like creatures scamper through the hole in the back of the cabin and crawl out the window. Unable to comes to terms with what may have just happened to her ex, she sprinted away as fast as she could, leaving their abrupt clicking, shrieks, and cries behind her. At the edge of the park she heard a large splash, and she turned around to see all fifteen creatures dive underneath the black surface of the pond.

Larissa raced as fast as she could through the otherwise tranquil suburb. She had royally messed up, and she knew it. Unintentionally unleashing a pack of bloodthirsty fiends upon the human race added up to an epic failure on her part. Coming to a rest, she bent over, thoroughly winded. All the Sunday morning jogs in the world couldn't have prepared her for this. Her chest thumped to the point where she thought it might explode. She didn't know where to run to, but after catching her breath, decided home was the best option. Warning Carter was top priority, but once aware of the messy state of affairs, he might also be able to help.

Larissa flew in the back door and then quietly hurried upstairs, thinking it unwise to wake her father until absolutely necessary. She burst into Carter's room. "Carter!" she half-whispered upon finding the empty room. "Where are you? We've gotta get out of here!" Larissa searched the closet and under the bed.

There was no sign of her brother and his video game was shut off.

Two miles away, the creatures reemerged from the pond. Antennae sprouted from the head of one creature, and it laid them on the ground, tickling the cool grass. The beast then emitted a series of squeals and took off in one direction, obediently followed by the others. The creatures maneuvered briskly in the night. Hearing the sound of music, one climbed a tall ficus tree overlooking Brittany Welles' backyard. Another creature clambered up, and from their vantage point, they could see a male and female teen making out in an upstairs bedroom.

Not finding Carter at home, Larissa headed to Brittany's house, where the party was in full swing. Music vibrated through the windows. Teens were spread across the congested lawn, clustered in small groups. She nudged her way through the mass. Out of the corner of her eye, she thought she saw one of the cricket-like creatures scaling a tree at the side of the house. She did a double take, but couldn't spot it. Okay, she thought, now you're either panicking or having delusions.

Spying a skateboarder she knew, Larissa drew near. "Hey, have you seen Carter?" she asked, trying not to appear too agitated.

"No, not lately. What's up?"

"Nothing." Again, she thought she saw one of

the creatures climbing a tree out of the corner of her eye. Then she swore she caught a whiff of their putrid stench. Were her senses playing tricks on her? Pull yourself together now, she said to herself. Continuing her search, Larissa approached a clique huddled close together. "Have you seen Carter anywhere?"

"Not tonight," someone said.

Larissa then came to the front door, when suddenly, a half-empty beer can soared through the air, striking her in the forehead. She reached up to her temple, and then stared down at the drop of blood smeared on her fingertip. Glancing to the side, she saw Christy Carmichael flanked by three of her friends. Christy laughed a sloppy, drunken laugh. Larissa took a step in her direction, but before she could reach Christy, Melissa stepped in her path.

"There you are!" Melissa said. "I've been so worried about you. You haven't answered any of my texts."

"I'm... preoccupied," Larissa said coolly.

"I can't believe your dad let you out tonight. What's gonna happen? Where ya goin' to school?"

That's when Larissa noticed the wine cooler in Melissa's hand. "Can I have a sip?" she asked.

"Of course."

Larissa took the wine cooler and chucked it across the lawn at Christy, who blocked it with her arm. Immediately, Christy sprinted over, shoved Melissa out of the way, and seized Larissa by the collar. "C'mon, badass," she said. "Let's do this."

Two jocks stepped in to separate the two. The party immediately collected in a circle around the girls, who were on the cusp of erupting into a full-on brawl. The crowd chanted, "Cat fight, cat fight..."

Brittany pushed her way to the inner circle. "Stop it!"

At that point, Christy spat in her opponent's face. Larissa tried to lunge at her, but one of the jocks restrained her.

"Larissa, stop!" Brittany yelled. "She's not worth it. She's..."

Suddenly, a blood curdling scream pierced the night air. Everyone gazed up to the second story, from where it seemed to originate. Glass shattered, and the body of a male teen came crashing through the upstairs window, falling with a thud onto the damp yard. Then came another scream. The teens looked up to the broken window where a girl overlooked the crowd. "Oh, my God!" she shrieked. "Help me..." A tentacle from somewhere inside the room wrapped around her neck and yanked her out of sight.

Then came more screams, this time from different parts of the house. There were sounds of doors slamming, glass breaking, and furniture being tossed about. While half the crowd outside split, the other half remained frozen in awe.

The front door opened and a goth chick darted out. A tentacle reached from inside, grabbed her around the waist, and hoisted her back through the door.

"What's that on the roof?!" the skateboarder asked.

The remaining crowd looked up to see three creatures perched on the roof. Christy, Brittany, and Melissa all turned to flee, while Larissa slowly retreated, unsure of where to go. Inside an upstairs window, she saw a creature sink its fangs into a yuppie teen.

"Hey!" Carter yelled from behind her. Larissa turned around to see her brother pull up in his souped-up golf cart. "Where have you been? Get in here!"

One of the creatures on the roof motioned to Larissa and then turned to screech something to the others. Larissa hopped into the passenger seat, and the golf cart peeled away. The three creatures leaped off the roof and took off after them in pursuit.

Carter accelerated past the panicked teens dispersing throughout the neighborhood. Larissa looked behind at the three creatures closing in. "What the hell are those things?!" Carter yelled.

"Just keep moving."

One of the creatures pulled ahead of the others.

"Can't this thing go any faster?!" Larissa screamed.

Carter put the pedal to the metal and the golf cart lurched forward. As one creature neared the cart, Larissa reached back to a golf bag and retrieved a five iron. "He's coming!"

The creature leaped onto the back of the golf cart. "Holy Jesus!" Carter screamed, almost losing control of the vehicle.

Larissa swung the club, whacking the creature in the head. She swung again, but this time the creature wrapped a tentacle around the iron and flung it from the cart. She grabbed a putter, and thrust it into the creature's mouth. The thing choked. Then, the second creature jumped on top of the first, knocking it off the back of the cart, and leaped onto the roof of the vehicle.

"Oh, my God!" Larissa shrieked.

The street came to an abrupt end at an approaching intersection. Carter turned the vehicle to a sharp right, but due to the high velocity, the cart tilted to the side.

"Lean right!" Carter said.

Clinging onto the roof, the creature swung to the left and flew smack into the back of a stop sign. It collapsed to the ground with a thud. As Carter and his sister leaned right, the wheels returned to the pavement. The third creature now leaped onto the roof. Larissa pulled another golf club from the bag, but a tentacle reached down and grabbed hold of it.

"Do something!" she pleaded to her brother. The golf cart raced into a cul-de-sac.

"I'm trying!" Carter replied.

Carter steered the cart onto a lawn and towards a tree with a low hanging branch. The branch whacked the creature off the roof, but the cart went crashing through a wooden fence and onto the eighteenth hole of the golf course. With nowhere else to go, the golf cart plunged straight into a deep and mossy water hazard.

As the cart sank to the bottom, the Locke siblings floated to the surface. At the edge of the pond, the three creatures dove into the water. "Get out!" Larissa yelled. She and her brother paddled frantically to the side and hoisted themselves out. Glancing behind, all Carter could see was the shimmery surface of the water.

"What are they doing?" he asked.

"Catching their breath." Larissa said, pulling Carter along. "Let's go."

"To the pro shop!" Carter suggested.

"Yeah!"

The two sprinted in the direction of the club house in the distance. Carter retrieved a set of keys from his pocket, and while fumbling with them, his sister kept watch on the empty course. No creatures in sight. At last, Carter found the right key and inserted it into the lock. He pushed the door open, and the two hastened inside.

"What do we do?" Carter asked, bolting the door.

"I don't know. Hide."

Passing by the pro shop, they quickly snatched a number of overpriced items from the clothing racks. Larissa left her brother by the shoe department to enter the women's changing room with the idea of getting out of her soggy clothes and into some preppy golf gear.

Suddenly, a knock came at the front door. Larissa stiffened, unsure of what to do. An uneasy feeling bubbled inside her stomach. Snapping to her senses, she quickly finished dressing into dry clothes. The knock came again. Leaving the changing room, she peered around the corner to spy Carter twenty feet away, crouched behind a clothing rack. He peeked out a window, and then the expression on his face drastically altered. It seemed as though he recognized someone. He stood, and before his sister could stop him, he rushed to the door, unlocked it, and pulled it wide open. Scarface took a step inside. Larissa gasped.

"Oh, my God." Carter said. "This is so strange. I can't believe it's actually you. I'm your biggest fan..."

Two tentacles burst from the sides of Scarface's torso, wrapping themselves around Carter's body. He cried out as Scarface's mouth opened wide revealing two curved sprouting fangs.

Larissa sprinted from her hiding spot and swiped a tennis racket from the pro shop. She charged at the creature and swung the racket at its malignant head, detaching it from the neck and sending it toppling to the floor. The tentacles released Carter and scoured the floor for the missing head. Carter and Larissa raced to the back door, but upon opening it, they spotted two creatures scouring the parking lot. They pulled the door closed and locked it. "We're in trouble" Larissa said.

"Follow me." Carter took his sister's hand and led her to the cantina. They stealthily crawled behind the mahogany bar and hid in the cabinet space underneath.

Meanwhile, Scarface discovered his missing head and clumsily replaced it on top of the neck. Perceiving a scratching noise at the front door, Scarface found his way to the back door and let his fellow shape-shifters inside.

The Locke siblings huddled in the darkness of the cantina, shaking helplessly and unsure of what to do. Larissa couldn't help but think that the moment of her demise was quickly approaching. Once they find me, she thought, they'll certainly tear me to shreds.

Her mind instantly flashed to her father, who would likely lose not only his daughter, but also his beloved son. Larissa's heart ached to think of the anguish that awaited both her parents, and she hated herself for not being clever enough to outsmart her adversaries. Then she heard the sound of footsteps followed by a familiar voice.

"We're willing to overlook this whole incident, Larissa," Scarface said. "In retrospect, I think we've been a little hard on you. Perhaps we haven't expressed our appreciation for all you've done. Perhaps we can agree on a more appealing arrangement."

Larissa peered upward and saw the collection of liquor bottles neatly arranged in front of the mirror. Whiskey, gin, tequila, etc. She then remembered her mother's words. A White Russian is a drink, isn't it? Vodka, maybe?

From where the two were crouching, they could hear one of the creatures leap onto the bar, its tentacles spilling onto the floor in front of them. "Let's make up, shall we?" Scarface continued. "And work together." The tentacles probed the floor behind the bar. One touched Carter's leg, and in one fell swoop, it wrenched him from his hiding spot.

"Leave me alone! Carter yelled as the creature heaved him onto the bar. Instinctively, Larissa abandoned her hiding spot and snatched a bottle of vodka from the shelf. "Stop it!" she screamed, hurling the bottle through the air. It missed the creature, but shattered onto a ceiling beam, drenching the monster in vodka.

An agonizing wail exploded from the creature's mouth. The monster released Carter, sending him toppling to the floor. In the dim light, Larissa saw the creature turn black and disintegrate where the alcohol had touched the skin.

She immediately grabbed a bottle of whiskey and hurled it at the second creature. Again, the bottle smashed, sending the creature into a painful tailspin. It collapsed, writhing on the floor. Larissa grabbed a bottle of rum, but spotted Scarface swiftly exiting the bar. Despite Carter's bewildered stupor, he managed to pull himself to his feet.

"Grab some booze," his sister ordered.

After arming themselves with spirits, the Locke children soon found themselves marching home through the vacant streets. They peered into the dark shadows between the houses searching for anything that might leap out at them. Larissa still gripped the bottle of rum in her hand, while Carter clutched a bottle of mescal.

When the pair arrived home, they could see two police cars and an ambulance next door at Brittany's house. Officers interviewed Brittany and a handful of her peers.

"Should we say something?" Carter asked his sis.

"What's the point?"

They headed to the back door, so as to not arouse their father. As Carter gripped the door handle, a moaning sound stopped them in their tracks. They followed the noise to the garden, where nine creatures lay semi-conscious. Black veins pulsated visibly through their skin. They appeared emaciated and in pain. Scanning Brittany's backyard, Larissa noticed the keg and several beer bottles scattered throughout the grass. She took her bottle of rum, opened it, and dumped its entire contents onto one of the creatures who groaned in agony. Carter opened the mescal bottle and doused the rest.

As Larissa let her bottle of rum drop to the ground, a tentacle swooped from above, wrapped around her body, and yanked her with brute force into the air. Leaves and branches swatted her in the face as the tentacle hoisted her into the thickness of an avocado tree. There, she caught sight of a creature in mid-transformation perched on a knotty branch. Its body remained that of a large cricket, but the face was decidedly Scarface. "Help me!" she screamed down to Carter.

Scarface scurried across a branch, pulling its prey in tow, and leaped over the fence into the alley. Larissa hit the ground with a thud, knocking the wind out of her. The creature dragged her across the dirt and rocks toward a manhole. "Help!" she yelled a second time.

Larissa heard the gate to the alley open and saw a glimpse of Carter running toward her. Then with one spiny leg, Scarface pried the lid off of the manhole and hurled it at Carter, missing his head by mere inches. The creature dove into the manhole, lugging her behind him. Her head struck the edge of the opening as she slipped underground. In a miraculous maneuver, her arm managed to grip the top rung of the ladder leading down into the sewer. "Larissa!" she heard Carter yell as he rushed to the manhole.

The adolescent clung to the top rung with her frigid knuckles, the creature tugging at her from below. Looking up, she spotted Carter at the opening's edge holding out his hand to her. "Grab my hand," he pleaded. She reached up, but the creature yanked her into the blackness. "No!" Carter screamed.

The splash of the icy water running underneath the street sent shock waves through her body. Scarface propelled himself with great rapidity through the water. He submerged, pulling her completely underneath the surface. She peered up to see the light of the manhole disappearing, and struggled to hold her breath.

Soon, amid the shivery darkness a bright blue flickering light appeared ahead of them. As Scarface dragged her closer and closer, she perceived a circular round portal emitting intense pulsating rays. Bubbles escaped from her mouth as Scarface dragged her through the portal, engulfing the two in the blinding blue light. Once through, she blacked out and all was dark.

CHAPTER 11

Ten days later, the students of Westlake High dragged their weary feet home from school, just like every other day. Missing person posters featuring Larissa's photo plastered the telephone poles that they passed. Mrs. Sumi watered the flowers in her front yard. Life had returned more or less to normal for her after a three-day visit to the hospital for symptoms of shock. On the golf course, a somber Carter Locke caddied for a pair of elderly golfers.

Across town in the community room of a Lutheran church, Gary sat in a folding chair with a pile of missing person fliers in his lap. Surrounding him, a therapist and several other adults lent him an ear. "It's the not knowing that's killing me" Gary said. "I feel that if I knew something, anything, that I could move forward in some fashion. To mourn, or to cope, or to cling to a shred of hope. But right now, I honestly don't know how I'm going to make it from one moment to the next."

"What do you think about when you think of Larissa?" the therapist asked.

Gary smiled. "I think about how mad she can make me. I never thought that I could get so mad at anyone. But anger fades. Regardless of whatever front she puts up, she's just a little girl trying to find her way in the world."

Gary's ride home that day was a blur. When he arrived, he sat in the driveway for quite a while staring at the windshield in front of him. After retrieving the mail, he sat down on the couch and began to rummage through it when a surge of emotion overtook him.

His mind brought him once again to the moment when Carter woke him that night in a frenzy. "Larissa's been taken!" his child screamed. Upon entering the alley, four police officers were already staring down into the black manhole. Had his daughter fallen into the abyss? Brittany Welles was there too ranting on and on about monsters, giant insects with tentacles. Gary's first thought was that she must have ingested some sort of hallucinogenic drug. But when Carter backed up her story, the baffled father didn't know what to believe. Gary was a logical man who put faith in only what he could see with his own two eyes. He didn't believe in aliens, ghosts, or angels. And yet, his daughter was gone, allegedly taken by force. But by who? And taken where?

Adding to his confusion were the memories of his wife Roberta. He recalled that same panicked look in her eye that both Carter and Brittany wore that evening. He recalled first seeing it that day many moons ago when he returned from a business trip only to find Roberta in a frenzy, rambling on about things in the dark. Things that were quick. Things that appeared insect-like one moment, and human the next. Was there something to this story, or was everyone suffering from mass hysteria? Gary leaned toward the latter, but was beginning to wonder if maybe he should try to keep an open mind.

Back on his sofa, he closed his eyes and took a few deep breaths when the doorbell rang. He hesitated for a moment, loathe to engage in any type of personal interaction. However, when Gary finally coaxed himself to answer the door, he found his daughter, drenched and freezing on the other side. Gary immediately threw his arms around her and sobbed. "Sweet Lord!"

"Who's there?" Carter asked appearing at the top of the stairs. Upon seeing his sister, he rushed down to embrace her.

That evening, the neighbors noticed two police cars parked alongside the curb in front of the Locke house. Inside, Larissa sat on the couch with Carter on one side holding her hand and her father on the other.

Four police officers scribbled down notes. "So what's the last thing you remember, Larissa?" one of them asked.

"Sitting in my room," the teenager replied.

"And the next thing?"

"Waking up here on the lawn."

"And you have absolutely no idea how you got there or where you came from?"

Larissa shook her head. "I'm sorry, but I don't."

The police ordered a doctor to give Larissa a physical exam, and so taking a seat on Larissa's bed, the female doctor attached a blood pressure monitor to the adolescent's arm. Larissa fiddled with the thermometer in her mouth.

"How do you feel?" the doctor asked, squeezing the pump. "Any aches or pains?"

Larissa shook her head. "Just sleepy."

The doctor nodded and released the air from the device. "Your blood pressure looks good."

In the kitchen, Gary lit the stove and placed a kettle on the flame. One of the police officers stowed a tiny notebook in his breast pocket. "Please keep us informed if she remembers anything."

Gary nodded. "Do you think she's telling the truth?"

"Honestly, there's no point in guessing. I think in time, either her memory will return, or she'll decide that she wants to talk. And when that happens, we'll be very interested in what she has to say. Just make sure she gets some rest." The police officer extended his hand to Gary, who shook it.

"Thank you, officer."

Sunday morning, Larissa wrapped a towel around her wet body and studied herself in the mirror while brushing her teeth. She rinsed and then paused for a moment, looking over at the toilet. Snapping out of her reverie, she remembered her chores.

Brittany Welles leaned on her mailbox while watching Larissa empty trash into the plastic dumpster on the street. "Even though Mitch McQueen broke a couple of bones, nobody died, so they decided not to have a criminal investigation," the cheerleader recounted. "At the same time, all these stiff goobers from the government came down from DC and interviewed us for about a thousand hours. I don't know what they were expecting to find out. There was a rumor going around that they confiscated some country club security video."

"What about Lance?"

"That's very interesting. His brother found him later that night passed out in the back of the nursery van, which was completely trashed." Brittany studied her neighbor to see what kind of reaction the information would elicit. "When he woke up, he said he couldn't remember anything."

Larissa nodded, looking up to contemplate the pale blue winter sky. "The fact that he was probably stoned out of his gourd probably didn't help much."

Brittany shrugged. "Anyway, none our parents or teachers like us talking about that night."

"People don't like what they can't understand."

"That's for sure."

When Larissa concluded her task, Brittany wrapped her arms around her buddy. "In any case, I'm so glad my favorite neighbor is back."

"Me, too."

On Monday morning, Gary reveled in the simple joy of driving his two children to school. After a friendly chat, he pulled the Chrysler up to the curb outside Westlake High. Larissa grabbed her backpack and opened the car door. "I love you," Gary said. "Call me if you need anything."

"I will. Love you too."

"Where is my sister, and what have you done with her?" Carter bellowed from the back seat. Larissa smirked and rolled her eyes.

Gary drove away with Carter while Larissa made the trek across the parking lot to school. The students nearby watched her curiously when the morning bell rang. In mid-conversation with Anthony, Melissa noticed Larissa pass by and chose to follow her best friend. "Hey, so it's official. You're back for more torture," she said.

"Apparently. Although I'm supposed to have a talk with Mr. Miller this morning. Lucky me."

"You'll have to text me all about it. I'll see you at lunch, okay?"

"You bet."

Later, Larissa sat down once again across the worn oak desk from assistant principal Mr. Miller. "I cannot express how relieved we all are to know that you are safe and sound. You gave us quite a scare, you know. And, we feel that given the circumstances, starting a new school wouldn't be the best course of action for you right now," he pontificated. "And as far as your recent behavioral issues, I'm prepared to just wipe the slate clean. What do you think about that? A fresh start."

"That sounds great to me."

Mr. Miller stood and offered his hand to Larissa, and she rose eagerly to shake it. "We're happy to have you back," the administrator said.

"Thank you."

Mr. Miller turned to adjust the blinds on his window.

"Take care, Larissa, and please don't make me regret this."

Larissa parted her lips, but instead of Larissa's voice, the voice of Scarface came through. "I'm afraid you won't be seeing Larissa anymore." Two tentacles burst from Larissa's sides and wrapped around Mr. Miller's torso. Mr. Miller gasped as Larissa's eyes turned black and protruded from their sockets, the head transforming into that of the cricket-like creature. The beast opened its mouth and planted its two curved foot-long fangs into Mr. Miller's neck. After extracting a pint of the assistant principal's blood, the fiend let Mr. Miller drop to the carpeted floor. Taking its time, Scarface metamorphosed back into Larissa, and the creature then checked its reflection in the small mirror hanging on the wall.

Wiping excess blood from around its orifice, the monster closed its eyes and paused for a prolonged moment. Hyperventilating on the floor, Mr. Miller clutched his bleeding neck and watched the impostor take a deep breath and slowly exit into the arteries of the institution. When the second period bell rang, the hallway became a stampede of students rushing back and forth to class. Before heading to Government, the creature posing as Larissa gulped down some water from the drinking fountain. Youthful energy bustling around it, Scarface simply remained in a daze just drinking, and drinking, and drinking...

CHAPTER 12

A day after crossing through to the other side, Larissa's eyelids squinted apart to daylight. She found herself laying in a thick metal cage inside the mouth of a spacious cavern at the edge of a sea. The aqua blue sea from the other world.

She had a vague recollection of Brittany's party, the wild ride on the golf cart, and the confrontation in the cantina. As she became more aware of her surroundings, Larissa noticed a talon shaped needle withdrawing blood from her punctured forearm, filling a translucent sac underneath the appendage of a creature crouched just outside the cage. She leered at the beast, so far her closest and clearest look at one of them. Was it Scarface? Larissa couldn't tell. Once the sac filled to capacity, the talon retracted and the creature retreated calmly into the sea.

Pulling herself to a seated position, Larissa found a tiny plate of bizarre looking raw vegetables and a jug full of water next to the cell. Feeling a hole in her belly, Larissa grabbed a root vegetable and began to eat. It tasted like nothing, but she hoped it would diminish the gnawing sensation in the pit of her stomach. The water quenched her dry lips, and surprisingly tasted like water back home, if not slightly better. Scratching her arm, she inspected what looked like a constellation of fresh puncture wounds. As she finished the vegetables, Larissa contemplated the row of empty cages next to her own. Perhaps others like herself would soon be moving in.

Several days elapsed with a similar routine. What appeared to be the same cricket-like creature woke her early in the morning, withdrew her blood, and then disappeared into the ocean. About three hours later, it would return to repeat the procedure. Again a few hours later, the same thing would happen. It fed her a plate of raw vegetables and water twice a day, which seemed effective at keeping the teenager healthy enough to manufacture blood. Fortunately, because she didn't eat and drink very much, she didn't have to go to the bathroom very often. When she did, she dug a hole in the dirt floor of the cage; and when finished, she buried the evidence. As in the world Larissa hailed from, the sun would set and then she would be left alone to sleep undisturbed. The temperature would drop, so she could only sleep for a few hours before the cold would wake her. At that point, she had no choice but to curl into a ball and shiver while waiting for the sun to reappear.

She contemplated counting the days as they passed. Part of her deemed the exercise pointless, but on the other hand, there remained nothing else to do but stare at the walls of the cave and recollect past events. She reached through the bars of the cage and grabbed hold of a small rock. She began etching a hash mark in the ground each morning to count the passage of time. So far, four days had elapsed.

On the morning of day six, while the creature was withdrawing her blood, Scarface emerged from the sea in human form. He approached the cage without comment, bent over, and smiled at his captive for a long moment. "Look at you now, Larissa. I guess you're not as clever as you once thought." The girl responded with a dispassionate look. "Don't you wish you would have worked with us? Hmm? You'll have a long time to think about that. A long time indeed." Scarface motioned to the adjacent creature as it withdrew the needle from her arm. "My comrade here will be keeping an eye on you to make sure you don't misbehave again." Larissa then curled up into a ball at the bottom of the cage and faced the cavern wall. After realizing the girl wasn't about to dignify his comments with a reply, Scarface disappeared into the sea. That encounter amounted to the one and only time she saw Scarface in the other world.

Larissa grew despondent over the next several days. Initially, she thought someone would surely come to save her. A search and rescue team would discover the portal, venture through, and deliver her from this misery. Alas, as days passed, her hopes waned. She was left to face the reality that she would likely die in the cage, emaciated and ill. Unable to brush her teeth, they would eventually decay and fall out. Her muscle mass would diminish and soon she would no longer be able to walk. She would neither see the faces of her family and friends ever again, nor experience the comfort of a cozy bed and hot shower. And whenever she wasn't thinking of loved ones, she thought constantly of the food she would never again have the opportunity to savor.

Then on the afternoon of day ten, the sound of rippling water drew her attention to the sea. Much to her surprise, Dark Eyes emerged from the water and approached the cage. "Where have you been?" Larissa asked, sitting upright. "I thought you were dead."

"I've been in hiding," he replied. "You almost defeated them."

"Almost."

Dark Eyes looked to the empty cages. "If we don't stop him, there will be others like you."

"I'm not in much of a position to do anything about it."

Two tentacles emerged from Dark Eyes' torso and grasped onto the bars of the cage. With what seemed like epic force, the tentacles pulled the thick metal bars apart, creating a large enough gap to crawl trough. "Come with me," he said.

Larissa relied on her atrophied muscles to wriggle

out of the cage and make her first attempt in almost two weeks to stand on two feet. After teetering for a few seconds, she clung onto the cage for support. "Gimme a minute," she said sensing the blood circulate through her legs. "Where are we going?" she asked, striving to hold herself up.

"To put an end to this."

A pebble fell from the cavern above. Larissa looked up to see her guardian creature scurrying across the rocky ceiling. The monster dropped to the ground, and facing Dark Eyes, bared its curved fangs. Dark Eyes immediately mutated into a creature, and the two locked in a vicious battle.

Larissa stumbled away from the cage, fell to her knees, and crawled deeper into the cavern toward a small ray of light. Behind her the two identical-looking creatures screeched and wrestled each other into a tangled ball. On all fours, she advanced up an incline, at the top of which she found a crevice leading to daylight. Climbing through the crevice, Larissa came to arid land, where she managed to support herself on two feet and hobble away. After only a few yards, however, she came to the edge of a cliff which dropped into the rough sea. The only direction to go was behind her and up a hill, so she spun around and limped upwards. As she passed the crevice, a bloodcurdling shriek erupted from the cave. Something down there had been seriously injured, perhaps mortally wounded.

Climbing the hillside, she succeeded in reaching the summit. A three hundred and sixty degree view revealed that she stood on the peak of a tiny island, trapped with nowhere to go.

Frustrated and helpless, she shrank down between some jagged rocks and hid. The realization set in that whichever creature down in the cavern overwhelmed the other would ultimately determine her fate. An eerie minute of silence elapsed. Then, the sound of rustling nearby made her jump. From around the rocks, she saw the antennae of a creature tickling the ground. Then in one brisk motion, the creature leaped on top of an adjacent rock and looked her directly in the eye. Larissa gasped.

The creature swiftly transformed back into Dark Eyes. Larissa exhaled a sigh of relief. "We need to move quickly," he said, "or there could be others to contend with."

As they hiked down to the sea, Dark Eyes told her that the creature she knew as Scarface had vanished. No one knew of his whereabouts, but Dark Eyes remained convinced that Scarface would find a way to resume his master plan. At the water's edge, they took a step in the lukewarm water. Dark Eyes perceived Larissa's hesitation. "You ready?" he asked.

Larissa felt a pang of anxiety over the thought of passing again through the portal. However, the promise of returning home prodded her beyond any apprehension. Larissa grabbed Dark Eyes' hand and the two swam into the warm translucent sea.

After swimming several hundred feet, they dove under the surface and passed through the portal, the ring of intense blue pulsating light. Before they knew it, they reemerged in the frigid, rank darkness of the sewer. Dark Eyes knew which direction to take, and so after a short swim, they approached the ladder. Climbing to the top, Dark Eyes pushed the pothole aside, which brought them to the alley behind the Locke house. Larissa crawled out of the sewer, while Dark Eyes remained perched on the ladder below. It was evening and the post-sunset light veiled her hometown in grey.

"You're not coming?" Larissa asked.

"I'd be too vulnerable." he said. Dark Eyes grabbed the pothole and returned it to its spot, disappearing in the darkness underneath. Larissa was alone and soaking wet in Walnut Creek.

Larissa deeply longed to see her father and brother, who likely thought she was now dead. She passed through the gate and headed across the lawn, noticing that the light in the dining room was on. She was ecstatic to let them in on the news that she was still among the living, but as she neared the window, nothing could have prepared her for what she observed inside.

Gary, Carter, and a teenager girl who looked exactly like Larissa sat around the kitchen table eating dinner. They laughed, and appeared to be having a nice time. Who was this girl? As she asked herself the question to herself, she immediately knew the answer. Larissa took a step back and watched them, her mouth agape in profound horror.

Scarface had taken her place. Her family didn't

miss her because someone else had robbed her of her identity. If these creatures could disguise themselves as professional golfers, why couldn't they assume the likeness of a surly teenager?

Still sopping wet and freezing, Larissa retrieved the house keys still wedged in her pants pocket, entered the garage through the side entrance, and found some old clothes in a box that her father had been meaning to donate to charity. She was shivering, but happily unearthed two woolen blankets from the emergency earthquake kit. She huddled in the corner and thought long and hard about her situation. Scarface proved himself not only a dangerous adversary, but a resourceful one too. Plotting his demise would require a careful and thorough strategy. Any blunder could come with high stakes. Larissa had made the beast furious with her at least once already; if she made him angry again, he would likely show no mercy.

CHAPTER 13

Larissa decided to spend the night in the tool shed located at the south corner of the back yard, thinking this a safer option than in the garage where she could be more easily discovered. She brought with her the blankets, food, and water from the earthquake kit, and she planned to pass the dark hours meditating on how to destroy the monster that had taken over her life. Before she could think clearly, she had to eat everything stored in the earthquake kit, mostly canned and dehydrated foods. With her hunger more or less satiated, a swell of acute anger suddenly came over her. She couldn't recall ever feeling this enraged before, and it took great restraint for her not to stand and hurl rusty tools at the walls of the metal shed.

The following day, Larissa listened through the shed door as her father, Carter, and the impostor left the house. The tell-tale beep signaling the unlocking of car doors carried to the back yard, followed by the sound of opening and closing of the car doors. The engine started, and the sound of tires backing down the driveway and then accelerating off in the distance indicated that all was clear at last. Larissa could now venture into the house.

The next three hours passed with Larissa in the bath trying to recuperate from the past couple weeks. Afterward, the fridge fell victim to Larissa's famished assault. Although she felt like consuming its entire contents, she realized this may arouse suspicion, so only items she knew wouldn't be missed made the cut.

The adolescent then pulled some clothes from the closet and stuffed them into a brown paper bag. She would be hiding out, so supplies were necessary. She snatched a few toiletries, and then feeling sleepy, decided to take a nap on her bed.

When Larissa awoke, the low blue light coming in through the window offered her a quick sense of the time. She shot up in bed, listening to see if Carter or Larissa II had returned home. Thankfully, a lingering silence indicated an empty house, but she knew there wasn't much time.

Larissa quickly hopped on her dad's computer and signed into her e-mail account. She typed in Brittany's address and added the following message, "Remember that favor you owe me? Meet me in front of your house at eleven o'clock tonight. Do not reply to this e-mail." Then, grabbing the brown paper bag full of supplies, she slipped out the back door. Knowing she needed to disappear until evening, she vanished to the park to work out a plan.

In the crisp winter breeze, Larissa swung by herself on the swing set watching the sun sink below the pine trees. As she would reflect on her situation, the intense feeling of rage would return. It was not an easy task to calm her nerves and focus on a strategy. Being blinded by anger was what had resulted in suspension when exacting retribution on Christy, and if anything, she learned that she needed to be more crafty and less impulsive. Redirecting her attention back to a plan, one thing became increasingly evident; again, she needed help.

By eleven o'clock that night, Larissa had positioned herself in Brittany's front yard hiding behind an old oak tree. The second story window presented darkness, but at exactly eleven, a light switched on. The cheerleader peered out the window, and Larissa stepped out from behind the oak tree waving her arm. Brittany offered an awkward smile, and then grabbed her coat. Two minutes later, the cheerleader appeared around the corner of the house, tiptoed up, and whispered, "What's this all about?"

"Is there a place we can talk for a few minutes?" Larissa asked.

Brittany closed up the top of her coat around her neck. "Let's go around the block," she replied. "But just one block! If my parents find out I'm gone, I'll be in deep shit."

As the two girls circled the block, Larissa hastily recounted her story of the past two weeks. At first, Brittany kept her eyes fixated on the sidewalk, but then she looked to her neighbor from time to time, as if to gauge her credibility from the expression on her face. When they returned to Brittany's house, the two sat on the curb, and under the dim light of the street lamp, Larissa showed Brittany the scars on her arm.

"When you're in art class tomorrow, check and see if these scars are still on my arm. If they're not, you'll know I'm telling the truth." Brittany studied the wounds and nodded. This was a lot for her neighbor to absorb, and so Larissa wanted to give it some time to sink in. That said, Brittany had previously witnessed the creatures' wrath first hand, and so perhaps her story wasn't so farfetched. "Tomorrow, if you believe me and are willing to help, maybe you can give me a sign."

"I usually close my blinds," Brittany said after careful reflection. "I'll leave them open tomorrow night, and you'll know I'm with you."

"Deal."

"I better get back," she said. "Where are you sleeping tonight?"

"In the tool shed in our back yard."

"That blows," Brittany said. Then after a brief hesitation, she turned to walk back home.

"Wait," Larissa said. "I might need your help with Melissa. She and I haven't exactly been the best of buds lately."

Brittany nodded. "I'll see what I can do." With that, the cheerleader returned sluggishly inside. Larissa's mind raced, and so she headed back to the tool shed in an attempt to get some rest. Tomorrow was going to be a big day.

Larissa woke the next day with a kink in her neck. When she peered out the tool shed, the sun stood high in the sky and all lights in the house were off. Nevertheless, she took great care not be seen as she crept up to the kitchen window to peer inside. Just as she thought, the house stood empty.

The walk to Carter's middle school took about fifteen minutes. When the lunch bell rang, Larissa searched the cafeteria in hopes of finding her younger brother. When she finally caught eye of him, he looked back at her with a puzzled look on his face. Larissa waved him over, at which point he said a few words to his buddies at the table and headed her way. At a short distance away, Larissa could plainly see dark circles under his eyes. She read last night's events plainly on his colorless face.

"You look different," he said, giving her a once over.

"I could say the same for you. Lemme explain."

The two of them strolled around campus and she broke it him that the person he took to be his sister was really an impostor. At first he assumed an expression of utter shock. Then like Brittany, Carter reflected on the information in silence for a solid two minutes. "I figured something wasn't right," he finally said, "but I just couldn't put my finger on it."

"Have you been having bad dreams?" Larissa asked. Carter looked at his sister, almost ashamed, and nodded. "I'm coming up with a plan," she said. "But we need to be careful and do this right. You wanna help me kick some butt, or what?"

That afternoon Larissa again scoured the pantry and carefully took a few munchies for the evening. She hid in the tool shed until after dark, and when all the lights were out, she took a walk. Upon her return, Larissa saw the blinds in Brittany's window open, and she breathed a deep sigh of relief. Larissa prayed that she had been able to talk to Melissa and convince her of the truth.

Later that night, while Larissa dozed in a state of half-consciousness, the door to the tool shed careened open with a blistering clang of metal. Larissa bolted upright, fearing she had been exposed. Brittany Welles, bundled in a thick pink coat and baby blue scarf, stepped inside and knelt down beside her. "My God, it's freezing in here," she said.

"You scared the piss outta me."

Over the next half hour, Brittany recounted the eerie events that took place over the last few weeks, about the special government force that came to town, and the lack of physical evidence to back up everyone's uncanny stories. According to Brittany, the fact that all witnesses were under the age of eighteen, and that they had all been drinking, detracted substantially from any credibility the testimonies may have had. She relayed that as soon as Carter reported Larissa missing to the police, a thorough search of the sewer system ensued, but nothing turned up. Brittany continued her tale up to the moment when Larissa showed up at the front door sopping wet.

"That said," Brittany elaborated, "we could tell that something was different."

"How so?"

"Well, you weren't really yourself. You seemed..."

"What?"

"Happy. Nobody knew what you had been through, and nobody wanted to talk about it. We just accepted that you were different, and that was okay."

Larissa nodded.

"But the Larissa I sat next to in art class today didn't have scars on her arm. That I know for sure."

"What I'm about to ask you to do is dangerous."

"I figured as much."

"Did you get a chance to talk to Melissa?"

"Yeah. She's with us."

"Awesome," Larissa said.

"Okay," Brittany said repositioning herself on the floor of the tool shed, "now tell me about this badass plan of yours."

CHAPTER 14

Early the next afternoon, Melissa and Larissa's twin left campus for lunch. As they strolled down the sidewalk toward the liquor store on the corner, Melissa rifled impatiently through her purse. From behind a dusty Chevy in the liquor store's parking lot, Brittany and the real Larissa caught sight of them several yards away.

"So, mine's gonna be ready in two weeks," Melissa said cavalierly before pulling a driver's license from her backpack and handing the fake ID to the fake Larissa. "In the meantime, here. The guy said it's completely authentic. Completely. State seal and everything."

"Oh, yeah?" the impostor said dubiously while turning the plastic ID over in its hand.

"Yeah. You're Sonia Schwartz from Sparks, Nevada. You better memorize your info in case they ask."

"I don't know, Melissa. I don't think this is gonna work," the creature said.

"Trust me. Joanna has used hers, like, five times."

The two came to a stop at the front door of the liquor store. "Then why don't you get Joanna to do it?" the thing protested.

"She's got a dentist appointment today," Melissa replied convincingly. "I promised Anthony and his friends we'd have it after school. Don't make me a liar."

"Melissa, I don't want to have any more trouble."

"How are you gonna get in trouble? First of all, it's gonna work. Second of all, if he thinks it's fake, then he'll just confiscate it."

Larissa's twin took a long pause, peering through the window of the liquor store at the rows of glass bottles. "Well, let's get it over with then."

"That's my girl! Here's the list." Melissa handed over a ragged piece of paper. At that point, Brittany and the real Larissa, still crouched behind the Chevy, split up and went their separate ways. So far, so good, thought Larissa.

The creature pushed the door open to the ding of a bell. Inside, seven rows of alcoholic beverages collected dust underneath the lofted ceiling. Behind the counter, the clerk busied himself opening boxes and ignored the minor's entrance. The fiend took a careful look around and then headed towards the refrigerated section in back, where a plethora of wine coolers chilled on display.

By that time, the real Larissa had already passed through the parking lot entrance and was lurking in the Italian wine department, watching her twin's every movement through the mirror in the ceiling corner. The impostor took a peek at the list, and then looked back toward the front door, where Melissa wrapped her bike chain around the outside door handles. The creature furrowed its brow, and then sensed a presence, for it immediately spun around to come face to face with the real Larissa.

The teen reached into her back pockets and felt the two water pistols filled with Absolut.

"How'd you get out?" the evil twin asked. Larissa was taken aback by the voice of Scarface coming through what appeared to be her own lips. She gripped her hands around the pistol handles and positioned her fingers on the triggers.

"Hey!" the clerk yelled from behind the counter, apparently noticing them for the first time. "You got ID?"

The creature parted its lips and shot a twenty-foot long tentacle from its mouth, slapping the clerk in the face and rendering him unconscious. The tongue retracted back into the mouth of the beast, who then turned to face its nemesis. Larissa pulled the two water pistols from her back pockets, but just then, two giant cricket arms burst through the creature's sides, pinning Larissa's arms to the back wall. The creature then lifted her into the air, but immediately, Carter rounded the corner of the aisle with a water gun in his hand.

"Say hello to Mr. Belvedere." Carter shot vodka from the gun which struck the creature in the arms. The monster wailed as the cricket limbs cracked apart, dropping Larissa to the floor. At the shock of hitting the tile, the two water pistols fell from her hands, and when the creature saw her reach for them, it leapt with incredible strength over the aisle toward the back door. The creature attempted to push the glass doors open, but found them also locked with a bike lock. The beast mustered its strength to rip the doors apart, when Brittany stepped in front of the rear exit outside.

"Cocktails?" she said brandishing an alcohol-laced water Uzi.

The creature froze for a split second, and then it pivoted around to face the Locke siblings, who rushed with guns drawn. Two tentacles burst from the creature's body and hoisted itself up to the rafters. Carter and Larissa looked upwards to spot the twin travel along the ceiling, using its tentacles to swing from one rafter to the next. Two more tentacles burst from the torso, reached down, and wrapping themselves around some California reds, hurled wine bottles at the two. The Lockes quickly ducked behind the aisles as the floor became drenched in liquor and broken glass. Larissa's double metamorphosed into a cricket-like creature while swinging through mid-air. Approaching the front entrance, the creature spotted Melissa outside shaking nervously while brandishing a water rifle of her own.

Larissa tested her weapons, summoned her courage, and rounded the corner of an aisle, charging at the enemy. She aimed her guns in the air and unleashed a warrior's cry. The thing opened its mouth, shooting its tongue through the air and whipping Larissa in the side of the head. She fell against the rum aisle and landed on the floor in a daze. The creature let go of the rafters and descended on top of the young girl. Scarface opened its mouth, baring its curved fangs. She tried to aim her guns, but the creature pinned her arms down with its cricket-like appendages.

Carter took a bottle of Shiraz, smashed the top of the bottle, and dashed at the creature. The fiend, without looking, whipped a tentacle through the air and around the boy's neck, squeezing it tight. Although promising to remain outside, once Melissa and Brittany saw the state of affairs, they feverishly began unlocking the bike chains that barred the doors shut.

The creature bit into Larissa's neck, and she wailed in agony. Carter's face turned blue as he grabbed at the leathery tentacle around his neck. Melissa was the first inside, but Scarface immediately sent a tentacle her way to rip the water gun from her hands. It did not see Brittany coming, who crouched behind an aisle, aimed and shot the beast in the side with a round of Tanqeray. Scarface retracted its fangs from Larissa and screeched while scanning the room for the assailant. By that time, Melissa had already broken the neck of a bottle of Brunello and stabbed the monster in the back.

As the crimson fluid entered its body, the creature released a wild and deafening squeal. The tentacle choking Carter went limp, and the boy unwound the appendage from around his neck. Larissa loosened her arms, took aim at the monster's protruding black eyes, and doused them with vodka. The creature screeched as its eyes burst apart, drenching Larissa in a sticky fluorescent slime. Carter smashed the top off of a bottle of Pinot and stabbed the creature in the back with the broken glass. As the bottle drained into the torso, the enemy erupted in a volcano of rank green ooze, bathing Larissa from head to foot.

Later that Spring, life in Walnut Creek returned more or less to normal. Melissa and Anthony broke up when the latter received an acceptance letter from a tech institute over two hundred miles south offering automotive and mechanic training. Upon reconsideration, they reconciled and committed to making the following year's long-distance relationship work. The Westlake cheer squad grew increasingly busy with its regional competition, and so Brittany Welles and Larissa rarely crossed paths. Larissa did learn though word-of-mouth that the cheer squad elected Brittany to take on the role of cheer captain during her senior year, an honor she would commit herself to fully. That same week, a narc busted Christy Carmichael for possession of methamphetamines, and the authorities forced her to take the remainder of the school year off to attend rehab. The Sumis, after quickly recovering from their brief trip to the ER, welcomed their first grandchild into the world, and subsequently moved to

Seattle to live closer to their family. A divorced family purchased the Sumi house, and the eldest son quickly caught the eye of Larissa. At sixteen, his fuzzy black curls, shiny latte-colored skin, and relaxed attitude made him not only a treat for the eyes, but also fun to be around. And yet, his dry sense of humor stood out to her as his most irresistible quality. After a few brief conversations, the new neighbor promised to teach Larissa a few simple skateboarding moves. After eagerly accepting, she immediately had second thoughts, realizing that she now risked the possibility of making herself look like a complete dumb ass.

Academically, the Spring semester unfurled in an uneventful manner. Larissa maintained her grades and made a concerted effort to keep her nose clean of any trouble. When one of Christy's friends coughed up a loogie on her backpack in trig one day, she simply smiled and blew the girl a kiss. She understood that in moving forward, carefully choosing her battles would prove paramount. She didn't make any effort to avoid Mr. Miller, but conversely Mr. Miller seemed to intentionally avoid Larissa. Whenever the two found themselves within eyeshot, Mr. Miller abruptly switched directions and vanished as quickly as possible.

Theories still circulated amongst the student body of the mayhem at Brittany's party and the mysterious party crashers. Some avowed that space aliens had finally invaded, and others surmised that a mutated science experiment must have escaped from a nearby lab. After having demolished Scarface at the liquor store, the four young adults adeptly destroyed the market's security camera recorder. Larissa felt strongly that no good could come from the police tracking down the four assailants and demanding an explanation. Not to mention the threat of going to juvie for destruction of property.

In early May, Carter, Gary, and Larissa found themselves once again in the reception area of the Winchester Hospital for Mental Health. Larissa sat flipping through a science magazine, while Carter used his sister's pocket mirror to examine the peach fuzz that had recently begun to flank his upper lip.

Roberta had worked very hard the past month to convince her panel of doctors that she no longer suffered from delusions. Not only did she refrain from speaking of pungent nighttime visitors, but strove to obey all hospital regulations, and did so in a pleasant, cheerful manner. Regular visits from her family bolstered her mood and kept her connected to the outside world. "The medication works miraculously," she professed at her scheduled review. After a week of continued observation, the admitting physician ordered her release.

The thick double doors slid open and Roberta appeared dressed in her street clothes and carrying a purse.

"There she is!" Gary announced while rising to his feet.

"You're all a sight for sore eyes," Roberta replied. As Larissa's mother stepped into the lobby, her three family members engulfed her in one long, tender embrace.

On the way home, Larissa heard her father laugh

for the first time in over six months. Roberta looked over her shoulder at her daughter. "So what's new in your world, Larissa?"

"Oh, not much. Sleeping a lot better."

That night when the Locke parents finally turned in for the evening, Larissa brushed her teeth, her eyes drawn to the porcelain commode in the corner.

"What are you thinking about?" Carter asked leaning against the door frame. Larissa looked into the clear water and reflected for a moment. She realized that the future would yield an array of unpredictable challenges and stumbling blocks. One could certainly count on life to be a bitch in that regard. Did Larissa simply need to prove herself an even bigger and badder bitch?

Her brother edged toward her. "Do you think everything's gonna be okay?"

Larissa reached for the medicine cabinet, where she retrieved a bottle of rubbing alcohol. Twisting off the cap, she released a splash of the clear liquid into the bowl. Then, looking to her brother, she offered him a shrug. "I guess we'll just have to just wait and see."

The End